Transformed

by Sarah Rose

FULTON BOOKS, INC.
New York, NY

First originally published by Fulton Books, Inc. 2014

ISBN 978-1-63338-004-2 (pbk)
ISBN 978-1-63338-005-9 (digital)

1

Blair walked into the large home, unsure of herself like usual. Considering the obvious wealth of the neighborhood she had passed to get here, she was expecting to see elegant colors painted on the walls, with a clean, sterile smell in the air. Instead, she was greeted by the scent of burning brownies in the oven, and a bright yellow room that contained the pinkest couch she had ever seen. "I didn't even know they made pink couches," Blair accidentally said out loud. As she heard the words tumble out of her mouth, she turned red. The woman welcoming Blair in to her home smiled sweetly at her and remarked about how she had searched long and hard to find upholstery fabric of that color, and how she had spent nearly two weeks refinishing her grandmother's couch. Blair mused about why someone so affluent would spend so much time redoing something old when she could buy something new. Little was known about this woman, but it was obvious that the way she lived her life was different than anyone Bair had ever met before.

Her name was Lizzy. Blair had seen her around town a few times, almost always smiling and talking with somebody. She was wildly animated, talking with her hands flailing in the air. She made large motions to go with exciting adjectives. Everything was amazing, eventful, and thrilling to this woman. A beautiful, wide smile was nearly always curved on her face. One time Blair drove by her as she was walking by herself in the early morning. While Lizzy's smile was not as wide then her lips still sat in a happy curve. She looked peaceful and pensive, especially when compared her to the next woman Blair passed. This woman walked hurriedly, had a fierce look on her face as if she had just stormed out of the house after a fight with her husband. The woman looked miserable, as if that walk was the last thing she wanted to do that day. The contrast was unbelievable.

Another thing Blair noticed almost immediately about Lizzy was how she dressed. Her body was not fat, yet it was not particularly slim. However, every outfit she wore seemed to accentuate all the good parts about her. She was a beautiful lady. About ten years older than Blair. Her hair was cut in a stylish manner, the short kind of style that had spikes in the back. Even though it was a messy style, it always looked perfectly put together, especially with the thick headbands she wore most days. She often wore button-- down shirts, sometimes sweaters, with brightly colored dress pants. Blair had never seen her without a scarf creatively tied around her neck. It was a style she admired, and only wished she could pull off. Even her name, Lizzy, was trendy.

Blair pondered her own name. If you looked it up in a baby book, it will tell you the name means plain. Technically, it means the kind of plain like a field, but really, Blair felt the plain Jane version is a better description. Blair was thirty-two, an age that was not old enough to be old, and not young enough to be young. She always thought she had a boring style. She used to try to buy clothes that were somewhat similar to what Lizzy wears, but they always felt odd. About five years ago, she found a great shirt that she liked at K-Mart. Blair loved the soft cotton feel of the shirt and wore it all the time. A month later, she returned to K-Mart and bought every color of the shirt they had. There were eight colors, and to this day she still rotates them in such a way that she never even has to think what she's going to wear. Five years of wearing the same eight shirts over and over. No one has ever commented to her about it, except for her mother, who often offers to buy her other clothes. Blair always thanks her and politely refuses every time. She also has four pairs of the same exact size 14 jeans. Technically, she is proba- bly a size 12, but she loved the feeling of putting on the 14s and having them fit a little big. Oddly enough, wearing a bigger size of jeans made her feel smaller. Blair's hair is shoulder length, and almost every day it is put in a ponytail with a holder that matches the t-shirt color of the day. Her bangs always presented her with a problem. When pulled back, her forehead feels exceptionally big, but if she leaves them out, she always end up with wisps of annoying hair in her face. Her hair is a non-descript color. Some may call it dishwater blonde, but Blair really hates that description. It conjures up stinky, murky images—not exactly what a woman would like associated with her hair. Often, she just wished to fit into the blonde or brunette categories. Even her eyes are hard to describe with their greenish brownish color. All in all, Blair was just an average woman. The only thing she felt was particularly remarkable about her were her eyebrows. She was the only woman she knew that didn't have to tend to her eyebrows at all.

One time at a Mary Kay party, a former Miss Texas turned Mary Kay consultant shared with Blair how she would love to have perfectly shaped eyebrows like hers. Blair knew the remark was an effort to win her trust and encourage her to buy all kinds of cosmetic supplies, but she always smiled when she thought of that comment. If nothing else, she always would have her eyebrows to fall back on.

So, for plain old Blair, to walk into bright vibrant Lizzy's house, it was definitely out of her realm of comfort. They had moved to their new Tennessee home earlier that summer. Her family had moved from a town in North Carolina that was about three hours south. The house they lived in now was smaller than most in town, but at least twice as large as their former home. The first night here, Blair's family sat in the narrow hallway upstairs. Blair had commented how they had always felt annoyingly smushed together at the old house, but here, they craved it. The four-bedroom home they purchased had a nice feel to it. It's spacious, but still cozy. Blair's husband, Samuel has given her lots of creative liberty to decorate it. So far, all the walls remained tan. Well, except for the bathroom.

The bathroom downstairs is just a box of a room, containing a toilet, a small sink, a mirrored medicine cabinet, and the washer and dryer. There's very little room to even turn around in there. But with three children, a husband whose new job will be very time consuming, and the never ending to do list that a mom has, Blair just knew that she needed to make that room a three-minutes-of-sanity-at-a-time room, a special room. For that particular place, she picked a paint called Palisade Blue. The richness of the blue, mixed with a subtle feel of gray gave her a comforting feeling every time she walked in there. Whether it was to switch a load of laundry or to actually take care of bathroom business, she felt important walking into that room. It reminded her of a rich person's bedroom in a fancy home interior magazine. Nothing about Blair was fancy, but this bathroom, made her feel like a new person—a different person. She had deliberately left the walls blank. She wanted one part of the house to feel like a clean slate, not cluttered up by toys, pictures, memories, one part to just feel simply elegant.

Lizzy's house was much different than Blair's. From her exotically decorated living room, to the passionate pops of color in every corner, to the well thought about lighting, flooring, and other details that make a person feel comfortable upon entry. Blair didn't own a single throw pillow. Lizzy had four, just on the pink couch.

Lizzy welcomed Blair, and took her coat and hung it on an iron coat tree that was placed next to a bench in the front hall. The bench contained another three pillows. She motioned for Blair to have a seat on the couch, which was much more comfortable than expected. At that moment, Lizzy must have smelled the burning brownies because she took off running. She returned about three minutes later, apologizing for the smell and the abandonment. Her apologies were well received, especially since she carried a tray with a carafe of coffee, accompanied by Blair's favorite kind of coffee creamer, amaretto.

Just then the doorbell rang again, but before Lizzy could even make it to the door, three more women just opened the door and walked right in. It was quite clear by the way they entered that they felt very comfortable letting themselves in after the doorbell announcement that they had arrived. They kicked their shoes off in a haphazard manner. Two of them flopped their pretty fall coats on the bench, and one of them, wearing a hoodie and not a jacket, took her hoodie off, sat crisscross on the classy looking high backed armchair and immediately tucked her sweatshirt into her lap. She looked so comfortable, as if she belonged here. Blair noticed that she sat a book on top of her sweatshirt. "Oh my goodness!" she thought. "I came to Bible study, but I didn't bring a Bible." At that moment, she wanted to get up and leave. Blair thought to herself, "I have no business being here."

These women were obviously friends. They knew each other well enough to plop on furniture and to open the door and walk in. And judging by the fact that they all had nice leather Bibles that looked broken in, Blair was pretty sure they were much better Christians than her, too.

The only reason she had agreed to come was because she was desperate to make some friends. These last four months of being lonely, trapped with the kids all summer, setting up house and not knowing anyone, had been very isolating. The few times they had gotten out to go to the library or the town carnival, they had seen Lizzy at all of them. She was the first person Blair could recognize as someone living in their new little town.

Blair had been at the grocery store carefully deciding on a pineapple when Lizzy walked up to her three weeks ago. She introduced herself. She said she had seen Blair around and also said that she had noticed her at church the last two weeks. Blair's cheeks flushed as she remembered the awkwardness of church. The kids were noisy, unsettled. She hadn't recognized the new worship songs they had sung and she was convinced each and every person there noticed their family had been faking these songs. Samuel, Blair's husband, had been very adamant to wait on giving to the church until they knew if the doctrine was sound, so even passing the offering plate back into the arms of the usher empty handed made her want to duck underneath the chair. Yeah, because this church had chairs. No pews.

In some weird way the move had excited Blair spiritually. Their old church was just that, old. Blair had memories of her college years, where her faith in God was the foundation of her life. As time had passed, and the responsibilities of life had drained her, and more and more time had been devoted to meeting her family's daily needs, she, like most of their former church, had forgotten what it was like to live out faith. She was a Sunday pew warmer and only prayed when she remembered to, which usually meant someone near and dear to her was near death.

Originally, she had been really excited about trying out a new church, a new style of worship. But, the newness of it all made her uncomfortable. And now, for some unknown reason, she had let herself enter into yet another uncomfortable situation, a Bible study in someone's home—someone obviously very different than herself. Blair couldn't wait for the ninety-minute study to be over so she could run home. She was already forming excuses why she wouldn't come back next week. And she was planning convincing arguments for her husband as to why they shouldn't continue at this new church.

Resolving herself to the fact that she had to remain here for the next hour and a half, she decided to at least drink some good coffee to help the time pass. As she sipped her coffee, Lizzy discreetly slipped a Bible on to the couch next to Blair. Blair wondered if she picked up on her panicked gaze to the chair girl's lap. She smiled a humble thank you smile in Lizzy's direction, to which she mouthed, "No problem" in response and winked, and then giggled a happy little giggle as she sat down on the chaise lounge in the corner. One of the other ladies sat on the other end of the pink couch, leaving a comfortable amount of space between them, and the other one moved to the rocking chair. She threw the pillow on the floor and wrapped the throw blanket on the back around her shoulders.

Lizzy opened the group with a quick prayer, and then she said everyone should introduce themselves. Being the hostess, Lizzy was willing to start off the group introductions. She shared how she had two children who were in their freshman and junior years at a local college and how she and her husband had married young, at the age of twenty. She smiled as she mentioned her husband, and stated they were as happy as ever. The next in the group was Monica. Monica was about the same age as Blair. She was quiet, but seemed relaxed as she rocked back and forth in the wooden rocking chair. She shared about her one child, who was in second grade. She talked about how her mom and dad had let her move in with them three years ago. Her husband, who had been both physically and emotionally abusive for years, had abandoned them for a string of physical relationships with several women. Blair felt sorry for her, but at the same time she felt she had too much access of knowledge about the woman as she shared about the abuse she had endured from her husband before he left. Blair felt unsettled and wrong knowing this about her, yet the Monica shared with ease, despite her obvious sorrow. She seemed to have a deep amount of trust for this group of woman. Lizzy, once again, seeming to read Blair's mind, looked at her and gently said, "We trust each other in this group. What is said here never leaves here." Blair nodded in agreement, but quickly reminded herself that she wouldn't share anything too intimate about herself.

As the third woman in the group started talking, Blair realized that she would actually have to share about herself. Her heart began to race. She hadn't really thought about that. She had planned on sitting there, absorbing all the information and not even speaking. Blair realized she was caught up in her own thoughts and had missed the third woman's name. As she snapped out of her inner dialogue, she realized this girl had a lot of zeal. She was talking about a hiking trip she took with her husband last weekend. Blair was pretty sure she heard her mention something about seven miles. Seven miles? Hiking? With hills and stuff? Oh, boy. This girl's enthusiasm for life seemed to be a little much for Blair.

Monica smiled so brightly as she listened to the third's story. "Wow, Jenny. Who would have ever thought you would have bounced back this strong? Even cancer can't keep you down. I'm so proud of you, hon." At that moment, all the other members of the group teared up. Blair felt ashamed of herself. Why would someone's enthusiasm annoy her? She had never met anyone who had cancer before. Blair stared at her hands, afraid to look up. She wasn't sure if all the tears she felt in her eyes were from self-loathing or if they were forming because of all the other emotion in the room. Blair was pretty sure that this was the breaking point for her. She would not be back again.

The last woman to go before Blair was the woman sitting next to her on the couch. She had been very quiet up to this point. At first Blair thought she seemed sullen, but then she realized she was just pensive. She introduced herself as Kate. Kate looked right at her as she began sharing her summary of why she was at Bible study. "Today marks my year anniversary of coming to Bible study. I remember the first time I came, I was so nervous. I couldn't get over Lizzy's kindness to invite me into her home, and how honest and real each woman here was with me. It was the first time that I felt like I could share my love of the Lord and still be able to share my struggles with sin. No one here expected me to be perfect. Heck, the first time I showed up to Bible study, I didn't even have my Bible. Look at you, showing up all prepared." Blair couldn't take her eyes off of this woman, and she could feel a smile from Lizzy's direction being sent her way. Kate went on to share how two years ago she and her husband had both had life changing experiences and decided to follow Jesus. She was married to a man named Phil. Kate talked about how she and Phil had two sons, Jeff and Damian. They were a handful. Still, she had desired more children. She talked candidly about how hard they desired to have a baby and raise that baby in the faith. It would be a completely different life than either of them had, but they were excited, yet beginning to get anxious as they had now been actively trying to conceive for over eight months with no success. Every head, including Blair's, nodded compassionately as Kate talked from her heart. Her love for God was evident as she trusted him deeply to give her the baby she was desperately hoping for.

Blair realized that Kate was done talking, and it was expected that she should share something about herself. She looked around the room at Lizzy, Monica, Jenny, and Kate. They all seemed to have so much purpose. She took a deep breath and spoke with a wobbly voice. "Hi, umm, my name is Blair. I'm married to Samuel. We've been married since we were eighteen. We have Ava, who is eleven, Charlie who is nine, and Franklin who is eight. I love being a mom, but I especially love it now that my kids are older and love talking to me about real life things. Ummm, let's see. We just moved to a house on Williams Drive. We moved here four months ago for my husband's job." Suddenly, Blair realized that she had not said this many words to someone outside of her home the entire time they had lived here. That thought was so startling to her, and her lip started shaking the way it does right before someone is about to let loose with tears. "Unbelievable! I finally talk to someone outside of my home, and now I'm blubbering." Blair silently chastised herself.

The more Blair fought the embarrassment, the harder the tears fought to make their escape. Absolutely mortified, Blair broke down in deep, full body sobs, in front of a room full of people she didn't know. She had expected to hear awkward giggles from the women sur-rounding her. Instead, they encircled her, placed their kind hands on her shoulders, and Kate prayed out loud, "Father, please meet Blair where she is. We are excited to see how you are going to change her life. Amen."

Looking back now, Blair is sure that moment is when her trans-formation began.

2

The afterschool crowd had gathered outside the small elementary school that Blair's children now attend. She enjoys watching the moms who obviously have five years or maybe even a decade of friendship. They happily wave at each other when they drive up, then again when they get out of their vehicles, and of course, when the meet they give each other a friendly we've-known-each-other-forever hug. It made her smile; still she felt a pit of self-pity fluttering around in the pit of her stomach.

She could hear the bell ring, and everyone began to prepare for the flood of children that would spill through the doors. They always release the younger grades first, so she waited for about five minutes for her third grader Franklin to exit. Franklin is a bit of an artist, and even at his young age, he walks with his head in the clouds most of the time. Often, as he rides his bike around the neighborhood he will stop in the middle of the street, staring off into space dreaming up his newest creation in his mind. Blair feels guilty about Franklin a lot. She always seems to snap him out of his dreams with her impatience. He processes things with great thought, and Blair tends to snap to decisions quickly. Franklin is her most sensitive, insightful child. As he sees Blair and opens his arms for a hug, his smile sort of fades and a look of great empathy washes over his face. "Mom, have you been crying today?" he asked her, unaware of the weight of his question.

Before she had a chance to think of some socially acceptable response, Charlie walked through the door. Charlie looks just like his daddy. He's tall for his age. Actually he's closing in on Blair faster that a nine-year-old should. He's got thick, wavy hair, an impish grin, and eyes that are crystal blue with a bright blue outlining the edge of his irises. Unlike his momma, the boy fits into every desirable category. Even with the school change, Charlie has stood out these last few weeks as a very popular kid. He's been invited to play with lots of other kids after school, and last week he excitedly showed Blair a paper to sign up for the basketball team. Even though Blair makes quick decisions normally, she had been slow about this commitment. Most people sign their kids up without a thought to the money or the time investments involved. Since they were penny pinching right now, and she was nervous about any time spent outside the comfort of her home, Blair weighed this decision more than usual.

Finally, the sixth grade was released. As plain as Blair may feel, she would never have to worry about Ava feeling that way. From birth, she has had thick, wavy red hair. Not the red that is bordering on looking like purple either. Ava's is rich, orange, and it has a soft curve to it. It is the kind of red hair you could never achieve chemically. She is short for eleven, but her bubbly personality makes up for her lack of height. Even though she's on the brink of adolescence, and the tween years are notoriously difficult for moms and daughters, somehow Ava has remained sweet. Blair had heard stories about girls who had turned ten or eleven, and how their households had feared them. Ava, sweet, beautiful Ava, was rarely ever in a bad mood, and definitely not fear invoking to anyone in their family.

The three children loaded up in the car, and the family made their way home. Blair thought that since she had a particularly rough morning with Franklin that day, she should make a peace offering with his favorite snack. All the snack contains is a piece of wheat bread with a dollop of cool whip. Blair had always thought it was a disgusting snack, but her kids, asked for it at least once a month. Her family had named them snowy mountains.

Blair was baffled over the power a mom had in her children's lives. It was more power than she felt comfortable possessing. She nostalgically remembered the first time she had made those treats for her children. It was out of desperation. They had hit a particular low point in their finances. Usually, her children were used to great, healthy snacks like apple slices and peanut butter, or yogurt. But when Franklin was three, their family hit some hard times. They found themselves praying to be invited to other people's homes for dinner, just so they could save money on the grocery bill. Sometimes they would eat plain white rice with a can of peas over it for a meal. Blair had remained grateful during that time that her children were good eaters and seemed pleased with the limited fare available to them. Everything was fine, until one day little Ava looked at her mommy and said, "Mommy, remember when sometimes we used to have the cookies? I miss the sweet cookies."

Blair's momma heart ached and she wanted to give her Ava a sweet cookie. She missed the luxury of being able to make snacks like that for her children. Out of desperation, Blair walked down to the freezer in the basement. There was only a twenty pound turkey, which her mom had purchased right after Thanksgiving, and a tub of cool whip. Blair had taken the tub of cool whip upstairs, thawed it, and spooned some on the bread. The snowy mountain name seemed to make the dessert sound fancier, and the kids loved it. The rest had been culinary history.

Blair gave the children their snack, and then transitioned them to their homework time. The two oldest headed to their rooms to use their desks for a homework station. However, Franklin had to sit at the kitchen table while he did homework. If left to his own devices he will draw a replica of what his teachers car looks like, but no homework would be completed for tomorrow's homework basket. Thankfully, hard-to-steer Franklin only had three math worksheets to do. He focused exceptionally well on the first two, while Blair cut onions and peppers in long strips for the fajitas she was preparing for dinner. "I'm so glad this new job has provided a pay raise for Samuel, and things like fajitas can be on my menu plan again." Blair thought.

She had moved on to cooking chicken strips in olive oil and garlic when she heard Franklin take a deep breath. "Mommy, you were crying today, weren't you?"

There was no distraction to avoid answering now. "Yes, Frank, honey. Mommy was crying, but I'm all better now." He looked at her, tilting his head to the left. She could tell he was deciding if he really believed her or not. Finally, he gave in and decided he believed his mother. She was glad because it was mostly true. The women at that Bible study had encouraged her so much that day. And for the first time since moving, she really did feel like it was possible to be happy here someday. She just wished she could settle the uneasiness inside of her.

As Blair finished cooking the fragrant dinner, she was surprised to hear Samuel walk in the back door a few minutes earlier than normal. She straightened her apron, brushed wisps of hair out of her eyes, and walked back to greet him. He smiled immediately when he saw her.

"Hey baby," he said richly. They embraced for at least thirty seconds. If someone had been watching, it would have been an awkwardly long hug, but no one was, and they both breathed in the other's scent. Hugging him as he walks in the door on any given day makes Blair feel like, no matter what, everything will always turn out okay.

She took all his dirty lunch dishes out of his lunchbox and immediately put them into the dishwasher. She tried to think of how she would summarize her day to Samuel, but she came up empty handed. Blair figured the right words would come once the chaos of the evening had settled down. Right now she had to focus on dinner to serve, and then showers to facilitate, and the many tasks to oversee. She prepared for the myriad of questions. "Did you lay out your clothes yet? Is everything in your backpack? Don't forget your gym sneakers! Is tomorrow library class? Do you have your books?" She seemed to go up and down the stairs twenty times a night and the hassle in the evenings seemed endless. However, all five of them knew this was much better than the alternative, a morning meltdown.

Finally, at 9:08 p.m., all the children were clean, packed up, and prepared for tomorrow. Samuel and Blair steal a sweet smile and collapse on the couch. Samuel never says much, but it's always been evident that he loves Blair. Blair loves him the same and lives by the motto, "I may not be good at much in this world, but loving this man is my specialty."

"Nice dinner, Hun," he says. The look on his face changes to a more serious note as he stumbles over the next few words. "So, ummmm, Franklin whispered to me tonight that you were crying. What was that all about?" Even though Samuel's words are short and to the point, there is a lot of love behind them.

Blair struggled to figure out where to start. She told him about each of the ladies today. Samuel had met Lizzy once so he could at least picture her. She told him about Monica and her story. She also shared how Jenny was an overcomer of cancer. Still very ashamed and emotional about her quick judgment, Blair had skipped over the part. Then, she shared with him about Kate, and how she was someone who understood what it was like to walk into that group and how she prayed for me.

"She prayed for you?" he asked.

"Yes. I started to cry there," Blair admitted awkwardly. She was too embarrassed to admit to Samuel how much she really cried. Sometimes, she would draw a hot bubble bath, sit there, and let her tears fall and mix in with the bubbles.

"Why were you crying?" At first Blair thought he was annoyed with her, but then she remembered from previous conversations how Samuel hated missing her cues, and if he was annoyed, it was probably more at himself than at her.

Before Blair realized it, words just started pouring out. "This move has messed with me. I'm glad we are here, but today was the most I've talked to someone outside of this house in four months. When we moved everyone kept saying that we would Skype and it would be great. Well, no one ever Skypes us, and when they do they have to go in about three minutes. I hate the way I feel about myself since the move. I've never felt lonelier in my life. I long to spend time out with friends, to feel like I'm a separate person. The kids are older now, but this summer I felt like they were all toddlers again as they depended on me so much to help them adjust. Just like when they were younger, I feel like I don't know who I am."

Blair was pretty sure she didn't breathe the entire time she was venting. She just kept talking and talking. And Samuel, well, he kept listening and listening. As he listened, he continued to look down, as if he was praying while she ranted. Over the years, he's learned to be quiet and calculated when the moods would make an appearance.

The pause was thick in the air, and Blair was hoping a strong, caring arm would come around her and soft words would come from him to soothe her spirit. Instead she heard, "What are you studying at the Bible study?"

That did it. She was already overly emotional. She just wanted to be consoled, to be hugged, and be told everything would be okay. She felt as if she got an overly spiritual response from an overly analytical husband. She flew up, gave him a look that no one would ever want to be on the receiving end of, and began to yell. "Is that all you can say? Is that all you care about? What book of the Bible I'm studying? Really?" She began crying all over again.

She pounded her foot on each step as she raced to her room. Just like a pre-teen in a hormonal frenzy, she threw herself dramatically on her bed, and began to sob into her pillow. Replaying the moments downstairs, she was ashamed of herself, but still teetering on the edge of anger. She could hear Lizzy's voice in her mind. "During this study of Romans," she had said, "we will learn all about how to renew our minds."

Blair was angry at Lizzy for saying her mind needed renewing. She was angry at Samuel for being too spiritual. And she was angry at herself, because deep down she knew they were both trying to help her, and as usual, she was wrong.

3

That night, Blair never did come back down stairs. She kept thinking Samuel would be up any minute to try and reconcile, but the minutes turned into hours. It was well after midnight before he climbed into bed next to her. She was awake, but pretended to be asleep. Blair was still mad at him, and was filled with shame at her behavior.

Her emotions always seemed to get the best of her. They always had. From what she had heard from countless other women, and from everything on prime time TV, Blair was not alone. Blair had the justification perfected in her mind. "If I only have a blowup like this once or twice a month, and the rest of the time I am easy to live with, loving, and an ideal wife, I am okay, right? A girl just needs to break down every now and then."

She lay there and tried to excuse her behavior for a few minutes longer. As Samuel's breathing turn heavy and patterned, she knew it was safe to get out of bed without waking him. She went downstairs, turned on the radio to a quiet, instrumental station, and sat on the couch. The darkness seemed too overwhelming, so she lit a candle.

Without really knowing why, Blair began to talk to God. Actually, even God was unable to escape her mood that day. Blair yelled so loud in her mind that the crying started again. Sharing these thoughts with God did not make her feel even a lick better. Her nose was beginning to leak and her head had started to pound.

Blair remember an older gentleman at her previous church saying that sometimes we spend all our time yakking to God, and we never set and listen. Since, Blair was pretty much feeling rock bottom, she decided to give it a shot. She sat quietly, asking God to help her hear Him.

The candle flame bounced around, really no rhyme or reason to its dance. Blair took a deep breath and exhaled it so slowly that she felt lightheaded. Then, out of nowhere there was a stirring in her heart. Not actual words or anything, but a stirring that seemed to remind her that she was loved. And then, the verses from Romans 12 that Lizzy had read earlier came floating in to her mind. "Be transformed." "Be renewed." "God's will" Blair couldn't remember it all, but as God's words floated around in her mind, she knew that she owed Samuel a big apology, and the Lord too.

Blair stood up with a new resolve and walked towards the kitchen for a drink of water and some Tylenol. As she passed the dining room table she found an envelope with her name on it. Quickly, she opened the letter.

> Dear Blair,
>   I am sorry I didn't have the right words for you tonight. I know these probably are not the right words either. But, I believe God brought us here to do something new in you and me. I love you. I wish I was better at saying what I feel.
>   Love,
>   Samuel

Blair recognized that it probably took Samuel nearly the entire two hours to pen down his words from his quiet soul. She felt an overwhelming amount of love for him, and she ran up, and cuddled under the covers next to her strong, warm husband.

"Samuel, I'm sorry. I'm so sorry for yelling at you. I love you. And I want to know what God wants for us too. Please forgive me."

Samuel rolled over and kissed her nose, like he often did. He said, "I forgive you. I love you." And, just like that, things were okay again.

Next up was apologizing to a God who obviously loved her

enough to give her a man like Samuel.

The next morning, Blair woke up with what she called an emotional hangover. Her eyes were encircled by a triple ring of gray, puffy ovals and the whites of her eyes here bloodshot. She realized that she had never even brushed her teeth last night and was grossed out at the particular vile scent of her morning breath.

Samuel woke up and immediately kissed her with a kiss that said so much more than good morning. It was full of promises of forgiveness, hope, and the reassurance that we were okay. Last night's gratitude for him was spilling over into her morning thoughts and she smiled, despite the remnants of the headache she had given herself the night before.

Thankful for all the preparations made last night, the morning routine went smoother than it normally did, and everyone was up, dressed, and out the door in record time. Now that the house was quiet again, Blair decided to actually reread the verses that Lizzy had read yesterday.

Blair grabbed her Bible, and sat down in the pose she saw Jenny take yesterday. Blair often found herself mimicking others' mannerisms. When she saw Jenny sit like that yesterday, she found herself admiring the spirituality and the trendiness that Jenny had demonstrated. Blair pondered if her behaviors were odd, or if other people did the same type of things. Pushing aside the thoughts, she flipped through pages upon pages of the Bible, struggling to find the book of Romans. She found it, closer to the back than it was in the front, and then she scanned the Bible book for the big number twelve.

"Romans 12," She said aloud, "Verses one and two. Therefore I urge you brothers in view of God's mercy to offer your bodies as living sacrifices, holy and pleasing to God—this is your spiritual act of worship. Do not conform any longer to the patterns of this world, but be transformed by the renewing of your mind. Then you will be able to test and approve what God's will is. His good, pleasing and perfect will."

Those verses felt very overwhelming to Blair and she felt relieved that Lizzy had just decided to study two verses that week. The phrase about offering her body as a sacrifice seemed very odd to Blair. Hadn't

Jesus already done that? However, as Blair read on, she thought about the part where they were not supposed to conform to the patterns of the world. She pushed that thought out quickly. She did not want to feel any more guilt. She decided to put the Bible study away since her to do list seemed longer than the book of Romans anyways.

She casually stood up and tried to rid her mind of the thought all together. It wasn't working. As she headed to the kitchen to fill her crock pot with a roast and veggies, she had another thought flash in her mind. One of the sitcoms she had watched a few nights before had been filled with naughty jokes, jokes that had made Blair laugh loud and often. She was starting to get the feeling that letting God in her life in this new way may be more difficult than she thought. And maybe not all she had hoped it would be.

Blair really hated feeling guilty. As she reflected over her behavior last night towards Samuel, she realized that most people who knew her casually would not even realize she was a Christian. Lizzy had mentioned that in Bible study the day before. "If people were looking in your windows of your house, could they tell you were a Christian?"

That entire conversation Blair had kept her head down. She remembered one time at her old job when a lady she had worked with for two years had tried sharing the gospel with her. Blair blushed even more when she remembered the harsh tone she had responded back to the lady, "I don't need to be saved! I've been following Jesus for ten years."

The lady had been super gracious to her. "I'm sorry, I didn't know," she then said, in a sweet way, not an accusatory tone that Blair had probably deserved, that she was glad to know that she had another fellow sister in Christ.

Blair had been furious. How could that lady not have known that she was a Christian? Looking back now at the patterns of the world that had a deep hold on her, it was quite obvious. That lady didn't know Blair was a Christian because Blair hadn't lived like it. That thought stabbed at her heart.

The guilt that Blair had been carrying around from her past, combined with her newly added transgressions made the burden she felt very heavy. Typically, Blair tended to get defensive when she felt the thick buildup of shame, but this time, that wasn't there. It was just a feeling, a knowledge that things needed to be different.

Next up on the never ending to do list was laundry. Two overflowing baskets needed folded and Blair was delighted to see that one of the baskets was towels. They folded up easy and always looked nice and neat on the shelves. Truth be told, towels were the only thing Blair was really good at folding. Everything else looked as if it had been balled up by a three year old. Thankfully, Samuel didn't mind that. Like Blair, he was just happy that things were in the correct drawers, and perhaps they could find them when needed.

Even though folding laundry was never the highlight of her day, Blair did enjoy that chore in some sense. It was a time to process and think about her day. As she folded, she started making a mental list of all the ways someone could tell she was a Christian. "I go to church. I don't lie. Okay, scratch that one. I'm lying about lying. Okay, um, I don't yell at my husband and kids. Oops. That isn't happening either. I love others and I don't judge." Automatically, Blair felt conviction as she replayed her initial judgment of Jenny yesterday. "I'm failing," Blair said, the heartbreak of her voice echoing in the empty living room. "The only thing I'm kind of good at is going to church, which I'm pretty good at thinking of reasons to get out of that too."

Blair was crushed. She really did love Jesus. And she had trusted in Him for salvation. But, the sheer fact was that there was not a lot of evidence or commitment backing those statements up. The thought shook her. And she did the first thing that came to mind. She called Lizzy.

Lizzy, true to the persona she puts off, showed up at Blair's door within fifteen minutes. She had a cup of chai latte for both of them. Since it was a nice September day, they headed to Blair's shady back deck to sip their lattes and talk. Blair began sharing her experiences with Lizzy. She told her about her argument with Samuel, and how she had been crying and convicted and just down right miserable. Then, taking a deep breath, Blair said, "I'm just awful. I'm so sinful. And no one, not anyone, anywhere would be able to tell that I follow Jesus the way I have been living lately. Not even lately, just like, forever."

Blair braced herself for what was coming next. She was sure there was going to be a list to adhere to from here on out, a list of rules to get back on the straight and narrow, instead, Lizzy truly surprised her with her response. She said, "Blair, when God gave us rules to follow, it wasn't so we would live a perfect life. He knew we could not do that because of the sin nature in all of us. Instead, he gave us rules to follow for our own good, and more importantly to show us how much we need Him. Even the Ten Commandments show us how much we need Jesus. No one I know has ever kept all ten of those. Even the easy ones like not murdering and not committing adultery, good people mess up on." Blair took a deep breath, as Lizzy looked at her with big eyes, full of hope and she said, "God will forgive you, and if you ask, he will help change you."

They talked a little more about Blair's doubts and fears and then ended by Lizzy praying. Lizzy asked Blair if she would like to pray and she shook her head no. This was all so strange to her. Here she was, praying with someone on her back deck! Her life sure had started looking a little different already.

4

Monica was always happy to get a phone call, especially when it was from one of her Bible Study friends. Lizzy was calling to ask her to pray for Blair. Monica was glad to have another member of their little study group. She did not have many friends, and her core group of friends was based around Bible study. So, when Lizzy asked Monica to pray for Blair and the spiritual issues she was facing, Monica was super happy to pray. In fact, she prayed with Lizzy before they even hung up the phone.

As they hung up the phone, Monica smiled. She loved being part of a group that so actively cared for one another. These women had accepted her when she felt her most unacceptable. They loved her, even though she was divorced, and a single mom. They never judged her based on her past. Despite the growing divorce rate, it always surprised Monica how much people made assumptions about her not trying hard enough in her marriage. It broke her heart when people looked at her in pity. She did not need pity. Even though she had been hurt badly, cheated on and abused, she was a strong woman, with a beautiful daughter. Her walk with the Lord was resilient, and it was all because of the tough circumstances she had faced in her life before.

Monica wished, however, that she was a little bit braver. If she were more courageous, maybe she would have been able to tell someone the latest news in her life. For the first time in years, Monica had a date.

About three months ago, Monica had decided she was tired of being lonely. She believed she was a woman who was well suited to be a loving wife to someone. Yes, she had been hurt before, but that didn't mean that God thought she had to be alone for the rest of her life, did it? So, without telling anyone, she made a decision to sign up for an online matchmaking process.

She laughed out loud as she rubbed her hands together excitedly. Actually, she even clapped and stomped her feet a little out of excitement. It felt juvenile to use the computer to meet someone, but she had been so excited! The hope and the wonder of what could really come out of it intrigued her. She had fun thinking about romance, and dates, and dolling herself up. To dream about falling in love again, just to dream about it, was enough to make her giddy. Her stomach jumped with nerves, and her heart pumped faster as she had filled out the form. She shared her age, her name, her body type, her beliefs, and an endless series of other questions. She prayed that her profile would not be deemed unmatchable.

It was about two weeks later when she received an e-mail of interest from one of the site's members. Monica was a substitute teacher for Mandy's school district and had not been called in that day. She had completed her morning tasks early and with ease. With the extra time, she decided to hop on the internet to see if anyone had viewed her profile. Seeing the e-mail in her inbox caused her face to blush and she was amazed that someone was actually interested in her.

His name was Jerome, but according to his message, everyone just called him Jer. He lived in the same town. He went to the big church just outside of town. He was very vocal in his profile about his faith and reading the e-mail Monica felt excited to meet him. At the very bottom of the email was his picture. Wow. If he looked anything like his picture, well, just wow! His boyish smile combined with his strong jaw line and clean, trimmed goatee made him one of the most handsome men she had ever laid eyes on.

Monica had a habit of telling herself, "God's got this under control." She often did that several times a day, even if she struggled to believe it at times. She felt like saying it out loud to herself was a reminder to quit worrying so much and believe God could actually handle what was happening to her. She whispered that phrase as she agreed to e-mail back and forth with him and get to know him better.

They had been e-mailing back and forth for a while now. They had enjoyed chatting about everything under the sun—their favorite music, their past times, and their childhoods. It was oddly easy to be open to someone while chatting online. She felt like she knew Jer better in just a few weeks than she had ever known Deke, her ex-husband. It both thrilled and scared her. Last Monday, she had received an e-mail from Jer asking her if she would be ready to meet him in person. He respected the site's safety policy and said that they should meet in a public place for their first time meeting. They had agreed to meet at a restaurant on the north side of town. It was a fancy restaurant, one with lighted palm trees and cloth linens. Each table had its own candlelight as well. Monica was nervous about the cost of the place and the high society feel, but Jer assured her in his e-mail that everything would be fine. Monica, a simple girl, had never envisioned herself in a place like that, but she was willing to try anything once.

She had really stepped out of her comfort zone asking her parents to watch Mandy for her. She had simply said she had wished to meet a friend on Saturday night. Her parents would have demanded too much information if the word date would have been used. That was only the third time she had asked them to watch Mandy since they had moved in two years ago. She was always afraid of being an inconvenience to them, even though they constantly reassured her that they were happy to be such a big part of their lives, and they were even happier to make sure that both Monica and Mandy were safe. As it turned out, they were thrilled to have some alone time with their granddaughter, and had planned to do pizza and a movie with her; that made Monica relax even more because she knew that Mandy wouldn't be missing her as she went out that evening.

Monica had decided that it was time to share the news with her Bible study friends. She asked God for wisdom and courage and prayed that she would receive the support from her friends that she had hoped for. Now, all she had to do was pray her way through today, a rainy Monday.

Even though the Monday weather was bleak and the day itself is not on the top of many people's favorite days, Jenny was in a great mood. She was driving to a job that she loved. She and her husband, Ryan, had spent all weekend having fun. Although she was sad that cervical cancer had ever wormed its way into her life, she was continually thankful for the new lease on life that it had given her and Ryan. Their marriage was stronger than ever. Their life, now that she was cancer free, was better than ever. And he truly was her best friend in the whole world.

Next up in her best friend line, was Monica. Jenny and Monica were so different. Jenny giggled out loud as she thought about how quiet and reserved Monica was, especially compared to herself, who was loud, excited, and perhaps a little too unreserved at times. Sometimes she would share a piece of information and wonder if she should have said it out loud. But, she was who she was. And that's what made her such a strong person with a positive outlook on life, and that was how she won that battle against cancer in the first place.

So many people would say things to Jenny about how sad it was that she could no longer bear children, but Jenny never really thought of it as a distressing thing. Before her diagnosis, she and Ryan were not sure if and when they would ever have children. They liked being open for ministry wherever God may take them, no matter what He may call them to. She liked being able to work part time as a physical trainer and still have plenty of money to go around. She loved being Ryan's girl and having him all to herself. She knew that sounded selfish to some people but it was just how God had made her, and she was thankful for that. Sometimes she did get just a little sad that the decision was no longer hers to make, however, she was glad to know the way that path would go in life. It would just be God, Ryan, and Jenny forever. And she loved that.

She always felt a little guilty when she considered how happy she was with her life, especially when she compared herself to Monica. Oh, sweet Monica. It wasn't that she wasn't happy with her life; it was just that she was so timid and shy about making big steps. Several times Jenny had thought that maybe she should try to set her up on a blind date. But, Jenny knew how private Monica was when it came to things like that, and she had not wanted to overstep the boundaries of their friendship.

Jenny had arrived at work a little early today. She was meeting one of her favorite clients, a morbidly obese man named Bill. Bill had been working so hard. Once weighing in at 425 pounds, he was down to 290. Jenny had worked with Bill his entire weight loss journey and every time they got to work out together, Jenny was reminded of the importance of her job, and why God crafted her to do what she did. She literally had a hand in giving people a new lease on life, and Jenny felt so thankful that God had entrusted her with that task.

While she waited for Bill to get there, she snuck into the back office to whisper one more prayer for her friends from Bible study. She knew from a phone call this morning that Lizzy thought Blair would benefit from prayer today. So, being faithful to her friends, even her new ones, she did just that.

Kate's Monday morning started out about the same way that every other morning started out. She and Phil had another fight. It was not that they did not love each other. They did, passionately, in fact. They just fought because, simply put, life was hard.

They had been married for fourteen years now. They had two boys, who Kate loved dearly, but to say the boys could get themselves into trouble seemed to be an understatement, especially recently. Damian, who was ten, seemed to get a note sent home from his fifth grade teacher at least twice a week lately, and Jeff, their eight-year-old had quite the mischievous streak too. Only in third grade, he had been suspended from school twice already, both times for fighting. The testosterone in her home wore her down often, especially since all four of them had big personalities and loud voices.

Most of the time, Kate just threw up her hands and said in exasperation, "Boys will be boys." This morning she had called on Phil for help. Apparently, that was a mistake. Phil, despite being the father, did not feel it was his job to address the situation with Damian's teacher. He told Kate that she should just handle it in whatever way she saw fit and call it a day. That started the two of them in a heated screaming match. They could never agree on how to raise their boys, especially since turning to God two years ago. This lifestyle was so foreign to both of them.

They wanted to live their life for God, and live according to what the Bible said. But, truth be told, life was easier when they paid a babysitter twenty bucks to hang out with the kids for a Friday night so they could hit the bar. Yes, life may have been easier in some ways, but Kate and Phil both knew they had made the right decision. They missed the bar and the friends that came with it, but she had fully embraced the acceptance she had received at the Bible study and at their church.

Since their life-changing experience, Kate had been able to transition from her waitressing job to her dream job. She was a painter for the local township. They always had murals or sketches that needed done. The work was not full time, but it was frequent enough to warrant a decent paycheck that was much bigger than her tips from the diner. She also loved the flexibility it had with allowing her to attend her daytime Bible study. Finally, some time that included women instead of three rowdy men. It added a small touch of femininity in her life, and a big dose of the Bible, which was just what Kate needed.

Kate was so excited to have Blair part of their group. She loved that she was not the newbie at the group anymore and she could welcome someone the same way she had been welcomed. Her heart broke for Blair when she started crying on the couch last week. Kate had been praying for Blair all week, so when Lizzy called to ask for prayers, Kate could say truthfully, "It's already done."

5

Blair arrived at Lizzy's a little early, just like the time before. When Lizzy opened the door, the familiarity of the place was comforting. Lizzy shared, "I hope you don't mind, but I called the other girls and asked them to pray for you."

Blair turned a little red, but shared how she was thankful for that.

And just like last time, the three other member of their little group showed up relaxed, happy, and thrilled to see one another. Blair could not believe how each member had shared the fact that they had been praying for her. She was humbled, grateful, and excited to learn from each one of them today. She whispered a silent thank you to God, who she was sure was smiling down at her, thanking Him for her new friends and her new attitude.

Lizzy had made some amazing cinnamon rolls to go with the equally tasty coffee this morning. Everyone oohhed and ahhed over the recipe and the chitchat was light and easy. Blair was amazed at how comfortable her second meeting felt with these women, even if she did not have a whole lot to add to the conversation. No one there had met her kids or her husband and that was all she had going on these days, outside of this little group of new friends.

After a bit, Lizzy suggested they get move to the Bible study. "Romans 12:3 is what we will be reading and working through today." She mentioned that the verses could be really challenging to work through.

While they were very powerful, sometimes they took a lot to apply effectively.

Blair had some very sharp thoughts pass through her mind. "Really, you say this Bible study stuff is hard, huh? " She hated when sarcasm took over her thoughts. She knew she did it when she was feeling defensive, and she tried to stop it, but she often found herself remarking unkindly to those around her, if only in her mind. She really wanted to be a sweet person. Why did sarcasm have to go and ruin that for her?

They read the verse together. "For by the grace given me I say to every one of you: Do not think of yourself more highly than you ought, but rather think of yourself with sober judgment, in accordance with the faith God has distributed to each of you."

"Well," Monica chirped in right away, "I think I may have this under control. I'm definitely not all high and mighty about myself. I know how many bad decisions I make each day and how I'm not perfect, nor have I ever pretended to me. In fact, sometimes I think that everyone else in the world is better than me."

Everyone pretty much nodded their heads in agreement. But, Lizzy, in her wisdom, mentioned a new perspective on the verse that no one had thought of. She brought out how it says to have sober judgment. Sober judgment was viewing ourselves appropriately. It was more than not being all high and mighty. It was about seeing ourselves through the eyes of grace, the way God would see us.

Each woman mulled over that. The room was so quiet and the women were pensive except for Jenny. Even though she should have been thinking about the answer, she was imagining thought bubbles hanging over the heads of her thoughtful friends. She finally got a hold of herself and when the laughter subsided, the group decided they had thought enough. They talked about how sober judgment would look in their own lives, and how improper views of themselves had really affected the way they lived. It infiltrated decisions much more than they realized. It was quite a discussion, and each person had a new, fresh perspective on herself by the time the conversation had finished.

After that was prayer request time. Monica's hands were shaking as she cleared her throat. It was time to ask her friends to pray for her!

As she had shared her emailing adventure with her Bible study friends, everyone seemed so surprised. Well, except Blair. Blair did not understand why this would be so shocking, but she also did not understand Monica's timid attitude towards men or taking big risks.

Jenny, always digging for details asked, "So, is he a hottie?" Everyone laughed and Monica turned bright red, but she nodded her head in agreement. Giggles continued as Monica told them the elaborate date planned for the weekend. She also shared her doubts and her nervousness. Each of the women was thrilled for her!

"What are you going to wear?"

"How are you going to do your hair?"

"Are you gonna kiss him?"

The questions came fast and hard.

Finally Monica put her hand gently in the air and said, "Woah! Slow down! I am freaking out a little bit now." They all felt a little bad for overwhelming her, but they smiled too, since this was just typical Monica.

Kate then began to share about her issues she had with Phil this morning. "Don't worry Monica," she said. "Not every relationship is as 'fun' as mine." They all chuckled a little, but they could hear the sadness in Kate's voice. Kate had shared before how she wished that she and Phil could overcome this part of their past. She felt like Christ had changed them in many ways, but they just could not seem to treat each other the way the Lord would want them to treat each other.

In her mind, Blair thought about how she wished she could even state the way she felt changed by the Lord. She felt so immature in her walk. But, thanks to all the girls praying for her and Lizzy's pep talk on the phone the other day, Blair just knew that change was on its way, as long as she kept trusting God for forgiveness and grace, and as long as she kept spending time with these incredible women.

They prayed for a few people that Blair did not know and then they decided to call the Bible study quits. Lizzy did encourage them to keep an eye on how they could actively try to have sober judgment throughout the week.

That evening Samuel, Blair, and the kids had a nice sit-down family meal together. They knew how blessed they were to have these moments together. Soon enough they would all find new, busy grooves at this home, and they wouldn't have as much time together. But right now, none of them had secured a lot of things into their schedule, or really found anything that would pull them away from the sacred dinner time ritual.

They worked their way around the table talking about homework, teachers, the kids the children were meeting, and Samuel's latest project at work. The conversation was mundane, but it was unifying. Samuel then asked Blair how her day was. The only thing out of the ordinary for her day was her Bible study. She shared with her family the lesson about having an accurate view of yourself.

Franklin, who always seemed to have something meaningful to add, even though he was the youngest said, "Mom, I know God made me an artist. I also know that I shouldn't brag about how good I can draw because I couldn't even do it if God didn't make me like this."

"That's good thinking, Son." Samuel encouraged him. Ava then went on to talk about what a good reader she was, and also how compassionate she was. And Charlie was so excited when he realized God could have made him athletic for a reason. Blair recognized that she had never made it a point to talk to her kids about God like this before. It was exciting and so different hearing her kids talk about God outside of the Sunday morning drive home from church. The family conversation was so edifying that even after dragging their feet another week about it, Samuel and Blair decided to give the okay for Charlie to use his athletic abilities for the basketball season this winter. It would take some sacrifices on all of their parts, but they knew that Charlie was a gifted athlete.

Already, Blair was counting down the days to Bible Study again. It was rapidly claiming many of her thoughts, and definitely infiltrating her life in a surprising way.

6

Monica could not believe how excited she felt. She walked with an extra bounce in her step. The week had passed by at what felt like a snail's pace. Finally, Saturday afternoon had arrived. The doorbell rang and she opened it only to find Jenny there. Jenny asked, "Do you think your parents would be okay with watching Mandy a couple hours early? I have a surprise for you!"

Monica hesitantly double checked with her parents, but they were delighted to have extra hours with Mandy all to themselves. Jenny directed, "Grab the outfit you are planning to wear and follow me back to my place." When they arrived, Lizzy's car was parked outside. As they walked in to Jenny's comfortable, midsized home, Monica was amazed to see nail polishes, lip sticks, eye shadows, curling irons, straightening irons, and even facial masks and a wax hand soak all arranged in stations around the kitchen.

Jenny went on to say how they could not imagine sending her out without giving her a little mini spa day. Monica smiled at her friends' thoughtfulness. They knew how rare it was that Monica did anything for herself. For the next hour and a half, they had fun like teenage girls. They ate M&M's, they talked about dates from the past, and they even wove prayer in through the time together, especially as the time grew closer and Monica's nerves were getting the best of her. All this commotion had caused Monica's imagination to get away from her, and she found herself dreaming of a future with this man she had never even met in person. She wondered if it was okay even to contemplate marriage, especially since they had not even arrived at their first date.

After she was dressed and prettied up in a way she had never been before, Monica got into her little car, and drove to the other side of town. She arrived four minutes early, which seemed like the perfect amount to her. As she was walking in the door, she looked through the glass. She saw a face that matched the profile. Jer's six foot two inch figure was much taller than she had anticipated. His presence was so comforting, so handsome, so overwhelming that she felt the heat rush to her face, making her face a sweet color of red by the time their eyes met. His smile made her feel as if she was losing the ability to think. The man was charming. Her heart was beating fast, and she had no idea how she would get her brain to actually form words in his presence.

He walked over and gave her a very appropriate, welcoming hug. He then stepped back, looked at her, and grinned. "You are even prettier than your pictures," he said. His voice shook as he said it, showing that he too, was a little nervous in her company. He was a gentleman, taking her jacket, pulling her chair out for her, and asking questions that relaxed them both.

After a few minutes, the nerves calmed down and it felt like they were old friends, which really, by everything shared in their e-mails, they were. They talked about Jer's work as a pharmacist, and Monica's never ending tales of what happens to substitute teachers. Monica had no idea she could feel so comfortable with a man. She felt like the filters that were usually on could be thrown aside. Whenever Monica brought up Mandy's name, Jer asked questions, smiled brightly, and seemed to care genuinely about her little girl. What a relief to know that a man like Jer would not reject her because of her past. Some men would consider Mandy baggage, but Jer seemed to think of Mandy as the blessing she was to her mother.

The dinner was amazing, cooked perfectly, and the service was the highest rate Monica had ever received at a restaurant. They decided to each order a piece of tiramisu and a cup of decaf coffee. When the dessert came, Jer's face changed a little bit. It no longer looked relaxed but very serious. Monica was nervous she had done something to offend him.

She noticed that he was trembling a little bit as he held his fork, trying to lift it up to his mouth. Finally, he looked at her, set his fork down with determination and said, "There's something I need to get off my chest." Monica sucked her breath in and held the air there, afraid of what would happen if she let it go.

"Listen, Monica. I'm a different kind of guy. I am thirty-six years old, and even though I've been single my entire life, I know what I want out of life and marriage. And, from everything I've learned about you through our e-mails and conversations, I believe you could be exactly what I've been looking for, you and your Mandy. I want to love you, provide for you. I want to be committed to you. I want to spend my life with a godly woman, and I just feel God's peace about this. I've prayed about it since the day I met you online."

Wow. Monica was stunned. "Are you proposing to me? On our first date?" she asked, very uncertain. After all, this man had not even met anyone else in her life. He had barely met her!

"No. This is not an official proposal, I'm just asking for your blessing to pursue marriage in the future with you, and much sooner rather than later. I want to build a relationship with Mandy, with your family, with your Bible study friends. I know this seems like a lot to ask in one date, but I know deep down in my heart this is what I've always asked God for. I just thought you should know my intentions."

Monica flashed a beautiful, big smile at him. She nodded her head. Inside her heart, she was thrilled. She had always dreamed of not having to go through another season of the dating game, and here, right now, in front of her, God was actively working this dream out. It seemed very out of the ordinary, but she was pretty sure things like this used to happen all the time back in history, even if they didn't have internet dating sites to help it along. She loved the idea, after all her heartache from her past with Deke, of being swept away in a whirlwind romance that had a solid basis. This was the best first date ever.

Kate and Phil had finally scored a babysitter. Finding a sitter for their sons was very hard. They had notoriety among teenage babysitters for the rambunctious behavior of Damian and Jeff. This was the first time they had been on a date in nearly two years. Was it any wonder they fought so much?

Earlier this evening, as Phil shaved and rubbed on a warm, musky aftershave, Kate realized that it had been a long time since she had even looked at him in a romantic light. He looked stunning tonight. He had on a deep blue colored shirt that matched his tie perfectly. She loved the sharp shoes he had on. He had a new haircut, and looked as excited as she did to be going on this date tonight. Almost every conversation they had anymore centered on the children and who should do what to discipline them this time. It was wearing on both of them, so Kate was surprised to find how attracted she was to Phil in this moment. It caught her off guard, and her heart picked up pace as she thought about having a dinner all to themselves, without having to yell at any-one.

Kate was a little jealous of the fancy restaurant uptown that she knew Monica was at right now, and Phil had even suggested going there earlier in the evening. Kate however, did not want to come across as nosey and look as if she was intruding on Monica's date (even if she DID want to see the new man!) and instead they picked a quiet family restaurant near their home. It was so close that they decided to enjoy the cool, crisp evening air and walk there. They kissed their boys good-bye, profusely thanked the seventeen-year-old girl that was naïve enough to watch them, and they stepped out. Both Phil and Kate took a big sigh as soon as the door latched. They looked at each other and laughed as they realized the relief of being on their own for once. Phil bent down and kissed her. Kate held on tightly to him in an embrace. She forgot that at one time, they did work very well together. There used to be more to them than just fighting and kids. A tiny spark of hope flickered inside of her.

As they walked to the restaurant, Phil shared how he was considering going to a Bible study for men at church. He said it was about being a man in today's society, being a loving husband, a dedicated father, and a strong leader. Phil sounded oddly vulnerable as he shared with Kate. The vulnerability increased as he said, "Kate, I'm sorry for the way we always fight. I know I expect too much from you. I know that I blame you for things that are my fault. I know I have messed up a lot in our relationship."

The first thought that passed through Kate's mind was "Finally, he's saying what I've been saying all these years." Then, Kate felt a sting in her heart. She knew she was being harsh and judgmental towards her husband who was just humbling himself right before her. She thought of the verse they had studied this week. In fact, she was so moved by the thought of it that she shared it with Phil. "Phil, God has redeemed us both. We both are under grace now. And, the fact of the matter is that there are times I blame you wrongly too, and I expect a ridiculous standard from you. Sometimes I think I just search for things to get mad about, just so we can fight because I have all this frustration with the boys built up."

"I'm sorry," they both said it at the same time.

"I'm really going to work on having sober judgment about myself Phil. I keep thinking I'm better than you, just because my ways are different. Our marriage will never improve if we continue on like this."

Phil smiled at her, his eyes full of forgiveness, and kissed her again. Then, right there, on a little cast iron park bench outside the restaurant, they sat down and prayed together and asked God to give them a fresh start. And an extra dose of patience for the boys God had gifted to them.

It had been a long time since Lizzy's phone had rung after ten o'clock. It was Kate on the line, just gushing about the amazing time that she and Phil had on the date. Kate shared all about the changes she could see coming up in her marriage and how much their Bible study had influenced them and helped avoid what could have been an all-out attack on Phil.

Lizzy commended Kate for her self-control. She told the girls all the time that it was easy to teach the lessons, but the hardest thing ever was to put it into action. She tried to be transparent in her teaching that she was not the best at putting things into action at times, but somehow she still felt like she was on a pedestal with these girls. She was amazed at how God had prompted Kate and Kate had responded just the way she should.

"Kate, God can transform your marriage! You just keep devoting time to God and one another and He will change you."

"Oh, Lizzy, have you heard anything from Monica and how her date went?"

"Not yet. Tuesday is going to take an awful long time to get here, I think!"

They said good night, and hung up the phone. What an exciting time it was for her friends! Lizzy was so grateful that they could each feel God working in their lives. And she was even more thankful that she knew God was in control in her life. She missed her boys now that they were at college, but she loved being where she was in life. She volunteered at the nursing home, she led the Bible study, and she even helped decorate the church for holidays. It was a blessing to be comfortable and stable. It was even more of a blessing to use that comfort and stability as a blessing to others. The girls did not know her back when her life was unstable. And even the people who knew her then never realized how terrible things were for her and Brad.

She looked over at Brad. He was wearing Tony the Tiger pajama pants and a white tee shirt. He looked relaxed, reading the comics on the recliner, and the cartoon tiger made her shake her head. Sometimes he was so silly. Things were so easy between them now. The stresses of child rearing had been great. She remembered how often she and Ryan disagreed over how situations should be handled with their boys. Flashbacks of arguments came back to her. She was not sure why it had never occurred to her to offer to watch Kate's boys, but she knew that her friend could use more moments like this with Phil, so that was exactly what she would do.

Then, she had a great idea. Brad loved being generous. What if they could send Phil and Kate away for a weekend?!? She knew money was tight for them, and she often heard of the never-ending babysitting battles. Immediately, she mentioned the idea to Brad, and he was excited about it too. Kate sat down at the dining room table and began to cut, color, and paste to make a little card and coupon detailing the gift she wanted to give her friend. She couldn't wait for Tuesday to come.

When Tuesday finally arrived, all the members of Bible study had so much exciting information to share with one another. Blair was amazed at the volume that five women could make.

The first order of business, after the cups of coffee had been poured, of course, was for Monica to share about her date night. She was nervous to share. Sunday afternoon when she had shared with Jenny, Jenny was happy for her, but seemed a little taken back by Jer's plan of marriage right way. Monica knew the idea of courtship was foreign to most people, but she had hoped for a little more excitement from Jenny.

Jenny had called her later that night apologizing if she came across as aloof. Sober judgment had infiltrated its way into her thoughts too. "Monica, I know that I may have one specific way of looking at things. Please forgive me for being so judgmental in our conversation earlier." It was easy for Monica to forgive her sweet friend. She knew that Jenny had her best interest at the forefront of her mind. Then Jenny did tease and say that she wanted to meet this man. "As soon as Mandy meets him, I'll have all of you over to get to know him."

So, this morning, before Monica shared too many details about the courtship, she proceeded with, "Then, he said something that you hardly ever hear another man say. I know it may sound different, but just hear me out." She went on to explain the courtship process that she and Jer had planned to use. She then asked for prayers because Jer was coming over this evening to meet her parents and Mandy. All the ladies squealed with excitement as they realized how big this was for their friend! Monica was grateful that the initial resistance she received from Jenny was not present here, and Jenny beamed a bright smile at her friend as she shared this time.

"So, when do we get to meet him?" Lizzy asked? Everyone laughed at the juvenile way she said it.

"How about some time next week? And, Lizzy, since you are so excited to meet him, can we all come over here?" Everyone laughed because they knew that in this group, Lizzy's house was the meeting spot for them. It would be quite a crew, and her house could handle the group.

After sharing the rest of their fun weekend stories, they opened their Bibles up to Romans again. Kate remarked how her Bible was opening up to that page almost automatically now. They all shared how easily that verse fit into their life this week. "Actually," said Jenny, "I wouldn't say it was easy to put into practice at all. It was humbling and put me in my place. But, it was easy to see how much I needed an attitude check." Everyone nodded in agreement.

Lizzy then said that they were going to work on a few verses this week. Blair raised her hand and said, only half joking, "If I have to work on more than one verse, my brain will hurt."

Amused, Lizzy assured Blair and the rest of the ladies that all these verses group well together, and everyone would be working on one main thought. "Find how you are meant to serve."

She cleared her throat and began to read the words from the Bible in front of her. "⁴ For just as each of us has one body with many members, and these members do not all have the same function, ⁵ so in Christ we, though many, form one body, and each member belongs to all the others. ⁶ We have different gifts, according to the grace given to each of us. If your gift is prophesying, then prophesy in accordance with your[a] faith; ⁷ if it is serving, then serve; if it is teaching, then teach; ⁸ if it is to encourage, then give encouragement; if it is giving, then give generously; if it is to lead,[b] do it diligently; if it is to show mercy, do it cheerfully."

It was hard for Blair to pay attention to the words Lizzy was reading. Jenny was practically flying out of her chair. She apparently really loved this passage. As soon as Lizzy had finished up by giving the address of the verses as Romans 12:4–8, Jenny broke in, "I know! I love this! I love that I'm doing exactly what God wants me to do. I'm changing lives, even though I don't work in a church or as a missionary. I'm helping people feel better about who they are and helping them achieve the things they have always wished they could."

"What do you do again?" Blair asked Lizzy.

Jenny went on to share about how she worked at the twenty-four-hour gym as a personal trainer. She told about how she felt that her physical fitness was a reason that she was able to overcome cancer and then she shared about Bill, her favorite client. Everyone was amazed as she shared her passion about fitness and eating well and making good choices for her body.

Blair mulled over a sentence that Jenny had said earlier about being used by God even though she doesn't work at the church. Blair remembered thinking about that before. If she wasn't a pastor's wife, a missionary, or even a Sunday school teacher, how could God ever use her?

Lizzy listed the gifts as she called them again. "Are you a prophet? What about serving? Do you teach, encourage, or give more readily than others? How about leading? Some people are so good at being in charge! What about showing mercy?"

Monica went on to share how she felt like she was a merciful person. She talked about how she was able to forgive things that most people would stew about for years. Everyone agreed with her as she talked about her gift. Blair wondered if everyone else was thinking about Monica's history with Deke like she was. How could a woman ever forgive someone that had treated her the way he had? Obviously, Monica was a very strong woman.

When Lizzy asked Blair where she thought she fit in, all Blair could do was raise her eyebrows. "I have no idea. I mean, I could do any one of those I guess. Well, I'm pretty sure I'm not a prophet," she said and everyone laughed.

Lizzy rebutted saying, "A prophet isn't just a bearded guy writing letters in the Old Testament. A prophet is a truth teller." Lizzy caught herself wincing as she said that last statement. The truth was one of Lizzy's toughest battles to win. She often caught herself lying about the stupidest things, and she didn't know why. Lizzy said, almost to appease her conscience, "Don't worry, Blair, I'm not a prophet either."

Kate shared how she felt that someday God may use her in a leadership role. Her life was just so hectic now, but she felt she did a great job delegating and organizing. Once again, everyone agreed.

Blair was quite disheartened because everyone seemed to have a place that they fit into, everyone but her. She prayed to God to ask Him for some help here. She decided to try to stuff the awful feelings away and talk to Samuel about it later. However, Lizzy decided that was not going to happen and broke in saying, "Blair, I feel like my gift is encouraging others and I want to encourage you right now! I know that I don't know you super well, but I want to tell you something I observed about you. You are a server. You take care of others. I've heard you talk about how you make sure your chores are kept up at home, how you make Samuel his favorite meals, I've even seen how you pick all our coffee cups up and take them to the kitchen after we are done with them."

"Ok. So I do stuff for other people. How is that important to God?" Blair was really feeling quite sarcastic and frustrated. She wanted to find out that God had some big plan mapped out for her in the great cosmic scheme of things. Not that she was simply supposed to be someone who swept floors and rinsed out coffee cups.

Lizzy said "I had a feeling you might feel that way. I want to share with you one of my favorite verses. It's from Colossians 3:23. 'Whatever you do, work at it with all your heart as working for the Lord, and not for men.' Do you realize that the way you serve others can be worship to the Lord?"

"I guess I never thought of it like that," Blair humbly replied.

Kate added in, "My pastor just talked about this the other day. He said so many people think his job is the big job in the church. And while he does a lot, he said that he would never be able to do it without people behind the scenes. He talked about those who watched kids in the nursery and the members who cleaned the church."

"When we serve in areas we are led to serve in, it frees other people to do what they are called to do. Not to mention it blesses others so much. Have you ever made a meal for someone else who was sick or just had a baby?" asked Monica

"Of course I have," Blair replied.

"Think of how much you have blessed that person, just by doing something that you are naturally good at," Monica encouraged her.

Blair mulled over the thoughts that her friends had shared. She wasn't sure that she felt truly gifted, but at least it had given her a fresh perspective on the things she did naturally.

By the time Bible study was over, Blair did feel a little more balanced. She thought about the things she did for her family every day and tried to consider how different it might look is she committed them to the Lord. The first thing that popped into her mind is that she may complain less.

That afternoon, as she folded a load of laundry, she prayed for her family. When she was folding Charlie's faded blue jeans, she asked God to protect him at football practice that night and that God would help him be a light to the basketball team he would be joining soon. She mated Samuels's socks and praised God for such a hardworking husband. She found Ava's favorite skirt tucked in the middle of the basket. Oh, she was so thankful for Ava's good attitude, her good grades, and her beautiful smile. When she got to the bottom of the pile, she found one of Franklin's shirts. Even though it had just come out of the washer, there were paint stains on it that were never going to come out. She was tempted, just for a few seconds, to be annoyed, but then she remembered this was about worshipping the Lord. She thanked God for her little artist and the gift God had given him. She was pretty sure she didn't remember seeing drawing and painting on that list in Romans, but she knew God could use Franklin's gift just as much as He could use her serving. And she truly was filled with a worshipful praise for her family and for her God who she was getting to know more and more every day.

7

Monica was nervous. Jer would be here at six o'clock sharp. She had so surprised at how well her parents had received the news of her date. Her mom hugged her and said she was so happy that she was willing to take that step. Her dad smiled at her and kissed her cheek warmly. They were always so kind to her. She wondered why she worried about upsetting them all the time. However, they seemed a little shocked by an idea of a courtship, especially when Jerome had not even met Mandy.

Monica and Jer had spent many hours talking on the phone since Saturday and they had a much better feel for how this relationship would work. Monica felt secure in the fact that they would not marry until Mandy and Jer had a working stable relationship. She shared that with her parents and they glanced skeptically at one another, but they had promised to remain open to the idea.

Jer arrived just before six. He wore a nice pair of khaki pants with a blue button-down shirt. Monica was so glad he had not worn a tie, since her dad preferred what he called a "man's man." Her dad thought men should be dirty, outside often, chopping wood and mowing lawn. Monica met him outside and they gave each other a big smile and a quick hug.

Monica's parents and Mandy were waiting there, right inside the door.

"Oh, Jerome, we are so happy to have you here with us tonight," Monica's mom, Nancy, said. He hugged her and presented her with a box of herbal teas wrapped with a little blue bow..

"Thank you for having me over," Jerome replied with a shaky voice. Monica had not even considered how nervous Jer may have been coming over here tonight.

"Jer, glad to meet you." Carl, Monica's father, reached out and shook the man's hand. They both eyed each other in a cautious way. Jer met his shake with a firm, respectable hand. They nodded heads to one another, a mutual sign of respect.

Kneeling down, Jer pulled a soft velveteen frog wearing a princess crown out of his pocket, and said, "And you must be Miss Mandy. I'm always hearing all about you from your Momma. She told me you like frogs, so I got this for you."

"Hi, Mr. Jer. Thank you for such a pretty princess frog! Momma told me you were coming tonight! I made you brownies that we get to eat with ice cream and fudge." She was smiling proudly as she pulled him to the kitchen to show Jer the pan of brownies.

Jer smiled at Monica and mouthed, "She's so cute!" to her. They wasted no time getting started on dinner. They were having a roast, grean beans, apple sauce, and a side salad. Everyone was enjoying the fare and the conversation. Jer seemed to instantly blend in with her family, which was rare, since few people were as old fashioned. They ate dinner together at the table every single night, homemade food, and desert included in that ritual.

They finished up the main course, and Jer was very helpful with cleaning up. That impressed Nancy a great deal. After they were done, Jer asked Carl if he would join him in the other room. He said they wouldn't need a long time. While they exited, Mandy just gushed about how strong Jer looked, how nice he was to her, and how much she loved her little princess frog. "Momma, he reminds me of a man who really loves Jesus."

Monica smiled at her and said, "Oh, honey, he does."

"What do you think Jer and Pap are talking about?" Mandy innocently inquired. As Monica thought about how the conversation may or may not be going, her heart did a little flip flop.

"Oh, probably man things" was the only response Monica could squeak out.

The ladies cut the brownies, scooped ice cream, and then drizzled both fudge and caramel on top. The sundaes looked divine, and Mandy was chomping at the bit to down her dessert. "Pap, Pap, are you done man talking in there?" she yelled.

Monica turned a little red, but Nancy laughed at the way Mandy said it. Sure enough the men came in the kitchen with big smiles on their faces. Monica was relieved to see everyone looking pleasant. She giggled as Jer gave her two thumbs up on the sly behind her dad's back.

"Pap, what man things did you talk about?" Mandy demanded. Carl looked at Monica, smiled and said they were talking about cars.

The conversation came even easier during dessert, and the four adults and adorable little girl talked until nine o'clock. When the big clock chimed, Monica realized that it was time to get Mandy to bed. Jer surprised her and asked if they could all pray together before Mandy went to bed. They moved to the living room and prayed a simple prayer that felt very natural. Then Nancy offered to get Mandy all tucked in so that Monica could have a proper goodbye.

Monica and Jer walked out to the front porch. The bricks on the front of the home were still radiating left over heat from the intense sunshine from the afternoon. She leaned against the wall since the air had become very chilly since sunset. Jer complimented her repeatedly about Mandy. He asked what she thought about the three of them going on an outing the following Friday. Monica said she would love nothing more. They glanced at one another, and for a moment, she felt that flutter in her stomach that said she thought he was going to kiss her. Jer broke up the flutter by saying, "As much as I want to kiss you right now, I'm not going to. I believe in walking the purest path possible, especially as we try to think clearly about where this is going." While Monica was let down by not getting a good night kiss, it was the most romantic statement she could have imagined in the moment. He was wholeheartedly seeking the Lord, even in moments when the world would have said a little compromise was okay. She loved where things seemed to be going.

"Jer, you are quite the man. Though this all seems to be moving fast, I can't believe how much peace I feel about all of it." Monica paused for a minute, deliberating over whether or not she should ask the next question.

She decided to go for it. "Hey, what did you say to my dad anyways?"

Jer laughed and said, "I'm not telling! All you need to know is he said yes!"

He teased her some more, they prayed together again, followed by a promise to call each other tomorrow evening. Jer said he was excited about Friday and would take care of all the details.

After Jer left, Monica floated up to her room and fell over onto the bed, just like a twelve-year-old girl crushing on a rock star. A big sigh escaped out of her mouth and she got so excited that she had to hop out of bed and wiggle the excitement out of her. She never imagined a man could make her feel like this again. What a mighty God she served!

Jenny and Ryan were settling down for the night. They had just read the Bible together and prayed for Monica and whatever would be happening over at her house right now with Jer coming over.

Jenny shared with Ryan how excited Monica had been. She also talked with him about how excited she had been when she realized how her position in life was a direct calling from God. I never realized how God could be honored so much in what I do. But, seeing Bill and others at the gym get healthy so they can live longer, that is such an honor. I love helping others, Ryan!"

Ryan smiled at her and said, "I know hon. In fact, I have an idea I want to talk to you about. It involves helping others." Ryan took a deep breath and said, "I want to be a daddy."

At first, Jenny thought Ryan was joking. Then, she looked at his face and saw that he was being very serious. "Ryan, what are you talking about? You know that isn't possible for us anymore. And we never even knew that was something we wanted even before I got the cancer?"

Ryan took a deep breath. "I know, Jenny. But, for the last couple of weeks I've been feeling like there's something missing from our life. We have plenty of money, an extra bedroom, and then, God confirmed it when I heard about it on the radio. Jenny, I really feel the need to look into the foster to adopt program."

Jenny was not sure how to make sense of everything he had just dropped on her. "Am I not enough? Do I not fulfill you, Ryan?" she asked with a dejected tone.

"Of course you are enough for me, Jenny. But, it's hard to explain. I feel this calling is from God, straight from His heart right into my soul."

Jenny was starting to feel a little angry. She had everything she wanted right now, a great job, a wonderful husband, and an adorable little house that was always nice and tidy. They never had to look for babysitters like all their other friends. They had more date nights in a month than most people had in a year. She loved being the center of Ryan's world, and it was embarrassing to admit that.

With a tear in her eye, she told Ryan she would think about it. She crawled under the covers asking God how this could be what He desired for them when, for her, it felt so awful to think about. How could that desire be growing in Ryan when it had never even crossed her mind? And how had he been turning it around in his brain for weeks and never even mentioned it before now?

Kate was amazed at how well the boys had seemed to behave today. Actually, they had seemed to be well behaved ever since Saturday when she and Phil had their much needed date night. It seemed easier to redirect them, especially since she felt like their parenting agenda was on more solid ground now.

They went to bed with only a few minimal squabbles about Damian getting toothpaste on Jeff's pajamas, but other than that, prayers were said and everyone did exactly what they were supposed to. It was actually quite blissful.

Kate had been anxiously waiting to open the envelope Lizzy gave her at the end of Bible study today. However, the way her day went, she had no time at all to open it, let alone read it. Her day had been busy running errands after Bible study. She picked up a package from the post office, bought veggies from the market, and then she had volunteered in Jeff's class the last hour of the day. The evening was a blur of dinner prep, clean up, homework and bedtime routines. She dug through her tote bag that she carried everywhere with her. It had her Bible, her wallet, her checkbook, permission slips, snacks for the boys, church bulletins, pens, gum—just about everything you could ever need was there. She always thought getting a bigger bag would be the solution. Wrong. It just fit more junk. She fumbled for at least a minute before she found the envelope. It was thick and smooth, bright teal in color. She opened the envelope and found a hand decorated card, filled with Lizzy's handwriting and encouragement inside. Kate could not believe the words she was reading. "Phil! Phil! Come read this!" Phil ran into the living room. "Read this, honey! Lizzy and Brad rented us a cabin this weekend. Oh my goodness. I get to go to the spa! There's a king sized bed and a hot tub! Is this really happening? And look! Right here it says that they are going to take Jeff and Damian."

"Woah" was all that Phil could say.

Kate called Lizzy just talking nonstop. "Thank you, thank you, thank you!" Over and over she continued to question the generous gift and give thanks back and forth. Lizzy was laughing. She didn't get to see Kate this excited very often.

Kate was so thrilled that she decided to begin packing for the weekend. She packed pretty pajamas that she never wore because she usually just fell asleep in an old t-shirt and shorts that she wore around the house in the evening. She packed nail polish and the prettiest dress she owned. She even thought to pack a notebook to jot down memories that she and Phil would make over the weekend. Suddenly, her life felt more like a fairy tale and less like the life of an overworked, worn- out mom.

It was Saturday morning. Monica and Mandy had slept in late that morning. The night before, just as he had promised, Jer provided them with a night out. They went to a miniature golf course before the sun set and the air chilled, followed by pizza and then ice cream. Mandy and Jer's relationship was growing quickly and Monica was encouraged with what she saw.

Mandy woke Monica up by crawling into bed with her. "Momma, thank you for letting me know Mr. Jer. He's such a good man. Maybe someday God will give me a daddy like him."

Monica did not say anything out loud to Mandy. She only prayed to God that Mandy was right. Monica realized that it was ridiculous to say this, especially since they had only met, but she really could see herself marrying that man. However, every once in a while, memories of Deke and their marriage would sneak up on her and make her doubt that any of this was really happening, or that there was any way of her having a happy ending.

Just Deke's name popping into her mind had made her uneasy lately. She remembered how things were with him. A memory came creeping into her mind. She remembered one time when Deke was upset because she had forgotten to change the clothes from the washer to the dryer. He called her a moron and lazy. He said she was worthless as a wife and a woman. Then, when Monica had begun to cry, he walked over to her, grabbed her hair, and slammed her head against the wall several times. "You deserve this. You don't do anything right. If you knew how to love a man, you would do things right around here."

Those memories always came back at the wrong time. It was Saturday morning. She and Mandy were supposed to have a day full of girly fun, and here she was tearing up over something that had happened nearly six years ago. Still, Monica couldn't help but wonder if Jer would ever do anything like that to her. When she first started dating Deke he was always nice, even if he had his temper flare up here and there.

Monica also wondered if she should share this past with Jer. She knew it would have to come up eventually, but the timing of it all seemed tricky. Jer knew she had been married before, but nothing more. What if Jer heard about what Deke had thought about her and it changed his mind about wanting to be with her?

Monica had to just push the thoughts out of her mind. Mandy was begging her to get up and cook breakfast. Mandy had asked for waffles and bacon, but Monica talked Mandy into having fruit and yogurt parfaits. They were healthier and they ate way too much junk food last night. Mandy, who tended to be good-natured and open minded, easily consented to the change of plans and she asked if she could cut and rinse the strawberries. As Mandy did her job, Monica rinsed blueberries and grabbed the container of homemade granola from the cupboard. She loved special moments like this with Mandy, the everyday moments. Just for fun, she decided to go back to happy thoughts and wondered what it may be like to have Jer be part of their Saturday morning. The wonderful thing about Jer was that he seemed to incorporate prayer into every moment he could. He joked and said that when you had lived alone as long as he had, you had to talk to God often because there was no one else around. Just thinking about his prayer life made Monica want more conversations with the Lord. She talked to God as she scooped the yogurt, lifting up Kate and Phi as they were enjoying a weekend away. She prayed for them to get to experience emotions like she had been experiencing with Jer over the last few weeks.

Since Monica had been married before, she was well aware of the fact that marriage was much more than just emotion and romance. However, because of the type of marriage she had been in, she was also keenly aware of how a little positive emotion and romance could be beneficial. Romance was a backbone that could provide hope in the darkest of times in a marriage. She wanted Kate to experience that hope so badly. Over the last year, poor Kate had seemed to be missing happiness in the worst kind of way. "Please, God. Please, give them hope. Let them see the best in each other and teach them to be kind and grace giving." As she prayed that prayer passionately for her friend, tears welled up, and she hoped that she would get the chance to live out a marriage again someday too. A marriage where, even if there were disagreements, she could be safe, and claim that hope for herself.

9

When Jenny's alarm went off on Tuesday morning, she was so happy it was Bible study day. She had been in a crummy mood ever since Ryan had brought up the adoption issue. For days she mulled over why Ryan felt like he had to mess with the status quo in their life. She was just happy to be alive. Wasn't that enough for him? Normally her attitude was nothing like this and she was frustrated at herself for being so irritable with Ryan. It was just such a big change in their life plan. And she was still reeling on how it came out of the blue.

That morning, Jenny slipped out of her silky pajamas and took the hottest shower she could stand. She took longer in the shower than normal. The water burned so bad at times that it was the only thing she could think about. She liked it that way because then she wasn't thinking about babies, or adoption, or cancer, or what a terrible wife she had been.

She hopped out of the shower and took her time getting ready. She blow-dried her hair, and put it up in a high ponytail. She decided she better dress for work because she wasn't sure if she would end up coming home after Bible study. She slipped on her favorite pair of black yoga pants. They fit just right and she loved the pink strips down the side. She put on hot pink socks to match with a layered look of a tank top and a zip up hoodie. She dabbed on some lip-gloss and a quick streak of eye shadow to add some girly feel to her outfit. She glanced at the clock and realized it was horribly late. She grabbed her Bible, her purse, and her keys and flew out the door. As she turned the ignition, she realized her gas light was still on. Hadn't she mentioned that to Ryan last night? Right before they started fighting again? Furiously, she texted Ryan. "*What? I thought I told you the car needed gas. Thanks a lot.*" She slammed the car into reverse and peeled out of the driveway. She sped down the road much faster than what was allowed in their little neighborhood. She slammed on her brakes at the end of their street. She looked left and right and then pressed the accelerator down hard, to the floor. She was so enraged, so hurried, and had to get to the gas station before Bible study. There was no way she had enough gas to make it to Lizzy's then work. As she completed the left turn, she heard a loud crash and felt the car spinning out of control. For a brief moment, everything went black. Though she could not see, she smelled the burning of brakes and tasted blood in her mouth. Her head was pounding and she realized that there was blood coming down her face, and tears too.

It was already 10:35 a.m. The girls at Bible study were anxiously awaiting Jenny's arrival. No one had talked to her that morning and it was very unlike her to be late. So, when the phone rang, Lizzy ran to answer it. Normally the phone would be sent to voice mail during Bible study, but with the nervous feeling they all had, she had to answer it.

On the line was Ryan. "She's been in a wreck. Please, please, meet me at the hospital. I have no idea what shape she's in. The police just called me."

Lizzy hung up and began to give orders while simultaneously praying. "Grab your shoes! Grab your coat. Please God, let our friend be okay. The hospital was only three minutes away from Lizzy's home, but it felt so much longer. They actually arrived at the same time that the ambulance did. The driver was clear that they could not see Jenny now, as privacy laws required family permission be given first. But, Lizzy noticed Kate staring over at the gurney, and both of them turned white as they saw how much blood was on the blanket covering Jenny.

Kate yelled, "We are praying for you, Jenny."

Meanwhile, Blair was just in shock. Nothing like this had ever happened to someone close to her before. She was wondering if she was going to be more of a hindrance than help since she did not know Jenny that well. In fact, she was so nervous about it, that she questions Lizzy. Lizzy looked at her straight on and said, "You are one of us now. We carry each other through these times."

Knowing that they only had to sit and wait for a while, they prayed off and on. After the women had been there for about fifteen minutes, Ryan arrived. He had driven from work, two towns over, in record time.

"Where is she?" Ryan demanded. He had been crying. "Lizzy was so angry at me before this happened. I think this may have been my fault. I hope she's going to be okay." Sobs poured out of the tall, strong man. Kate gave Ryan an awkward hug, and took him to the emergency room guard who walked Ryan back behind the big double doors that seemed more ominous than ever.

As Blair watched Kate pace back and forth, the sight of Monica caught her eye. Jenny and Monica were as different as night and day, but they had been best friends for years. Monica had her hands folded in silent prayer, but you could tell by the deep squint of her eyes, and how tight her jaw looked that Monica was incredibly focused. Feeling slightly uncomfortable, Blair slid over two chairs and put her arm around Monica. She wanted Monica to know she was supported too. As a few minutes passed by, Blair could feel the tenseness in Monica's shoulders relax and the lines formed around her eyes and mouth began to relax a little bit. Blair rubbed her back in a gentle caring kind of way and caught herself saying, "It will all be okay."

Monica opened her eyes and smiled with a twinge of hope. She quietly spoke to Blair. "I think there's something bothering Jenny. Before this, I mean. She's been really sad this week, and distant. I've been so afraid that the cancer's back. This was sort of how she was when the cancer came. Sometimes she would almost get mean towards Ryan, or sometimes towards me. I really hope that is not what is going on. She's been so off for the last few days."

They started praying again, not only for Jenny's physical protection, but whatever was going on to cause her to be distant. They also prayed for Ryan, and their relationship and whatever may be going on to distress Jenny so much. Time ticked by at normal speed for the world around them, but every minute was painstakingly slow as it crept by in their world.

After about forty-five minutes, Ryan emerged back from the world beyond the double doors. He looked worn, frazzled, and still plagued by tears. "The good news is that Jenny is expected to make a full recovery. The bad news is, it is going to take some time. She had pain everywhere, a broken collar bone and a broken wrist, not to mention cuts all over her body."

Treading very carefully, Lizzy asked in a maternal manner, "And how are you? And are you and Jenny okay?"

Ryan just gently nodded his head that things were okay. "You can go see her now. I gave permission for the four of you to go back. When Jenny heard Kate call out to her in the parking lot, she started begging incessantly for you to be allowed back. I'm going to go and find a bottle of water and get a little fresh air. She's all cleaned up now, so she doesn't look too bad. Just don't try to hug her or anything yet, since they don't have any casts or braces on her."

The four of them were given the okay by the security guard, and they walked to room number seven. They peeked around the curtain to confirm it was the right room and they found Jenny weeping. "So selfish. So selfish." She kept saying the words over and over.

Even Monica, who had walked through many hard times in life with Jenny, had never seen her like this before. It was a heart wrenching scene. The physical side of things was scary, as there was still blood in Jenny's hair, and she had marks all over her face. But, to see her berating herself so much, it was more than Monica could bear. Monica sat down against the wall outside the ER room, put her head down on her knees and cried. Blair sat down next to her, hugging her, while Kate and Lizzy went in. Very carefully, Lizzy reached over and held the hand on Jenny's right side, which seemed a little less beat up then her left.

Jenny looked right into Lizzy's eyes and said, "I'm an awful, selfish woman."

Lizzy looked right back at her and said, "There is no way that is true. You give so much to those around you. This is just a bump in the road. You focus on getting better. We'll help you through this Jenny. I promise, sweetie. You have us all here helping you." Lizzy's voice was teetering on the brink of tears too.

At that point, Monica came in, and she wiped away her tears and said, "Jenny, I don't know what happened today. But, I do know you are the strongest woman I know. You have never been awful. And we all deal with selfishness."

Jenny shook her head and said, "Not like this."

Everyone wanted to ask her what she meant by that, but they were afraid to upset her anymore. They sat there with their friend for a few minutes, until Ryan ducked in. He had composed himself a bit more, and he smiled sweetly at Jenny when he came through the curtain. "Honey, the doctor said you need to rest now. The pain medication works the best when you are resting." Ryan directed his conversation to the other women in the room now. "Thank you so much for coming, for being here for Jenny and me. I appreciate your prayers and the way you care for her. Please be praying for us. And if you don't mind, I think Jenny and I could use some time alone now."

All four nodded, and compliantly left. Since Jenny still needed the casts to be put in place, they simply blew kisses to her. They walked out of the hospital and stood on the sidewalk, next to a very full parking lot. Lizzy had a thought that all those cars belonged to someone who had a loved one in the hospital. Each car represented a hurting person. Sure, maybe a few represented a newborn baby, but most were there for sad reasons. It was an overwhelming thought.

"How about some lunch?" Kate asked. Without many words they agreed on a local sandwich shop. They ate, mostly in silence. Emotions were fresh and raw right now. Gratefulness was right at the top, being so glad that Jenny was alright, even if she was pretty banged up. However, they were all worried and highly concerned for their friend and how atypical she seemed today. What had happened to make her so distraught? Hesitantly, Kate asked about it. Everyone either shrugged their shoulders or shook their head. No one seemed to know what had happened to their friend.

"Okay, Jenny. Listen, hunny. Why don't you just calm down. Sweetie, shhh. It's okay." Ryan was growing desperate to calm his sobbing wife. All the crying and the emotions were not helping the situation at hand. His stress level was at a nearly all time high. First, getting Jenny's text, and then the police calling him at work, then filling out paperwork, and trying to work with the insurance companies, claims, and police. He was shocked to find out that the accident was deemed to be Jenny's fault. What in the world had happened?

Finally, Jenny dozed off to sleep and Ryan prayed over her incessantly. Because of how worked up she was, and the fact that she had just recovered from cancer, the doctor suggested an overnight stay would not be a bad idea. Ryan had readily agreed. While she was sleeping a sound, medicated sleep, they wheeled her into a private room. When Jenny woke up, she was much calmer and after a few tender kisses, and a bunch of I love yous Ryan cautiously asked Jenny what happened.

"Ryan, I was driving like an idiot. I was so mad at you. I've been so selfish. And apparently, it takes a car accident for me to see this." Jenny took a slow deep breath. Her head was throbbing and the last thing she wanted was for more tears to come and worsen the pain. "Ryan, I don't know how to tell you this. I'm just so ashamed. The reason I didn't want to have any kids is because I like it being just you and me. I love the convenience of it just being us. We have extra money, we have time together. Every weekend is easy and we do so many fun things. I didn't want to give it up." Another big sigh.

"This morning, I was so mad at you. Not because of the gas. Well, not really. But, I was mad because God was showing me your heart was in the right place. My heart isn't. Ahhh! It frustrates me how caught up in me I get sometimes."

"Shhh, Honey. We all do it at times. Don't be so hard on yourself." Ryan was trying to keep her calm. He was trying to keep calm himself, though tears were brimming. The way she was talking, it sounded like she may be softening to the ideas he so firmly believed were in God's plans for them.

"I've been reading ahead a little in our Bible study. It tells us to have sincere love. And to hate what is evil and cling to what is good." Tears began welling up and threatening to spill over.

"Ryan, my attitude has not been loving. I've been selfish. That's evil. I know it is. I need to cling to what is good. I know what you want for our family is good."

"Honey, why don't you rest? We will talk about this when you are healed." Somehow, his voice remained calm, but inside Ryan was thrilled. His Jenny was making a comeback. He opened the drawer that was beside her hospital bed. In the drawer, just as he hoped, was a Bible placed by the Gideons. He read her a few Psalms, and some from Romans, and then, the love chapter in 1 Corinthians. He thanked the Lord for a very clear picture of what love is, and was thankful that hopefully, very soon, they would be living with more love in their life.

10

The next morning, Lizzy woke up earlier than normal. Yesterday seemed like a hazy memory from years ago. Before opening her eyes, she prayed immediately asking God to take care of Jenny and Ryan. Her heart broke for her friends. Trials were part of life, she knew that much. But, still, it was miserable watching her friends walk through hard times. She didn't mind them for herself nowadays, but ten years ago, or so, when she was the age of her Bible study friends, she used to get all worked up about every little bad thing that happened. The more she studied the scriptures, the more she had come to realize that the tough things in life were what molded people into stronger, better people. It brought to mind another verse in Romans that said God worked everything out for those who love Him. But, there was another thing that Lizzy had learned. She shuddered as the thought hit her again. There were also consequences for our behavior. And while she didn't know exactly what Jenny was talking about yesterday, she imagined that somehow the accident was also a consequence of a poor decision, or maybe even a bad attitude. She tucked that thought back into her mind. Even thinking it felt judgmental. She would let God deal with Jenny on that. When people were hurting the last thing they needed were friends who said, "You must have had that coming." No, Jenny needed reminding of the goodness and the forgiveness of God, she needed reminded of grace. And she needed her friends' support to heal both physically and emotionally, so she could be held in the arms of grace. It was going to be a long, interesting road for all of them.

She got up, washed her face, drank a tall glass of water, and brushed her teeth. Lizzy decided what she really needed was time alone with God outside. She grabbed jogging pants, a hoodie, put in a head-band, and headed outdoors. She made her way to their housing development's park. It encircled a big lake, and the lake had a dirt path that people often walked or jogged around. Lizzy was captivated by the beauty of the morning.

While she had hoped she would be alone, there were two walkers there with their dogs. It seemed maybe they were a couple, and an odd couple at that. The lady, somewhere in her mid- thirties maybe, was petite, with long hair pulled back into a straight ponytail. She was walking an enormous St. Bernard. That dog seemed as if he may weigh more than she did. The dog was obedient and walked at a nice pace that suited his short master. Walking next to her was a man, at least six foot tall. He was wide shouldered, bald, and reminded Lizzy somewhat of Mr. Clean. Oddly enough, he was walking the tiniest little white snowball of a dog that Lizzy had ever seen. And the dog was frantical-ly running all over the place, pulling its ginormous master back and forth. The sight was quite humorous, and Lizzy actually startled herself when she laughed out loud.

Life sure was funny sometimes. She was glad God had opened her eyes to the humor around her. Yes, this was a tough time for her friend, but a good attitude would go far, not only for Jenny, but for all of them. She continued on her walk, looping around the mid-sized pond three times before heading back. She lapped the couple on her last trip around and wished them a fantastic day as she passed by. They smiled and wished her the same.

Lizzy thought she would call Blair to check in and see how their newest member was holding up. When Blair answered, she sounded worn out to Lizzy. "I just can't stop worrying about Jenny. She was so shook up yesterday. I want to do something, but I don't know what." Lizzy smiled and shared an idea with Blair.

When Blair hung up the phone with Lizzy, she felt so encouraged.

Finally, she could see how God could use her gift of serving to bless someone else. She sat down, began planning. She opened her laptop, started researching, and then she began making a list.

She paused for a second, and asked for God's help. "Wow," she said out loud, "I don't think I've ever prayed about something so fast before." Then, before she went any farther, she sent a text message to Sam. "Might need to dip into savings for an idea to help Jenny. I promise not to spend too much. Okay with you?"

"Do it!" was his simple response.

With Sam's blessing, Blair sprang into action. She went and changed into her color for the day yellow. She got her matching yellow ponytail holder, and started to put her hair up. She decided in honor of doing something new, that she would dress different too. Blair dug through her closet, and pulled out an orange fall sweater and put it on. And just for good measure, she put hoop earring in too. Wow. It felt good to look a little different. She tossed her hair around with her fingers and combed her bangs just right. Whew! What a difference a few little changes could make.

Blair first headed to the bulk food store. She bought foil and several disposable trays. She bought ten pounds of beef and fifteen pounds of chicken. She bought pasta sauce, noodles, canned veggies, cream of mushroom, and cream of chicken soups. Blair tried not to think about what the cashier must think about her buying all this food. It looked ridiculous, but Blair was on a mission.

After she loaded the bags into the hatch, she climbed into the driver seat. She clicked the button for the heated seat to turn on, trying to soothe her aching lower back, while she dialed Lizzy's number. "Lizzy, I got the groceries. Can you grab the crock-pots and meet me at my house in forty minutes? I need help unloading this car. My back is killing me already!"

Blair made a couple more stops to get a few fresh items, and then she grabbed take out for her and Lizzy. As soon as she got home, she began setting up a well thought out assembly line. They threw on aprons, started cooking meat in the crock-pots, chopping veggies, cooking down sauces, and printing recipes.

They continued working hard for a couple of hours. Prompted by the smell of the crock-pots hard at work, Lizzy's stomach growled loudly. "Oh my goodness! I forgot I got us lunch!" Blair yelled with amusement in her voice. They reheated the grilled chicken sandwiches and ate them quickly.

Another half hour of prepping and all the meat had cooked thoroughly in the crock-pots scattered around the house. Blair looked at the clock. She was so thankful that Samuel was picking the kids up from school, because it was now ten minutes later than she normally left to get them. They began filling the aluminum pans with lasagna, chicken casseroles, enchiladas, and shepherd's pie.

Samuel and the kids arrived. They tossed their backpacks and jackets aside and scrubbed their hands. With everyone helping, it took under fifteen minutes and they had assembled twenty-two meals for Jenny and Ryan. When Blair had picked out the tins, she had chosen smaller ones since it was just the two of them. Some of the meals made several of the same kind of meal, so there were repeats, but Jenny wouldn't have to worry about dinner for nearly a month! That would definitely help her recovery stress.

Just as they finished, Lizzy and Blair both got a text from Jenny. "Headed home."

Lizzy smiled and said, "You ready to go make a delivery?"

"Absolutely! Let's go!" Blair was so excited and her face shone brilliantly.

Samuel stared at his wife. She was smiling bigger than he had seen in a long time.

"Blair, you look so beautiful."

"Oh, it's the shirt and earring," she said quickly.

"No, Blair, look at me. *You* look beautiful, radiant. I love seeing you in the middle of a God thing."

And right there, in front of the kids and Lizzy, he kissed her to prove how much he loved her in that moment. She turned red, playfully hit his arm and said, "C'mon now. Why don't you help us carry these to the car?"

As they drove away, she caught Samuel's eye, mouthed, "thank you," and blew him another kiss.

Blair and Lizzy got to Jenny's house, shortly after she and Ryan had arrived. They first went in and greeted Jenny with warm hugs. Jenny seemed a little bit more like herself. Ryan was sitting on the couch, next to her, with his arm wrapped protectively around her shoulder. They were a cute couple, that's for sure. "Jenny, Blair has a surprise for you." Blair turned red and insisted that it was for sure a surprise from Lizzy too.

They told Jenny to stay put and then asked Ryan for some help. They carried in meal after meal. Jenny started to refuse the kind gesture, but Lizzy stopped her right in the middle of her argument. "Now, listen, Miss Jenny. We will have no stubbornness here. We all talked about our gifts at last meeting, and this is Blair's chance to let her gift shine. You need it, and so does Blair." Lizzy didn't mean to sound so maternal, but sometimes, her nature took over.

Blair beamed as she realized that God really could use her, just the way she was. And Jenny nodded with tears in her eyes as she admitted that Lizzy was correct. In fact, after a few minutes, Jenny was crying because she realized that her saying no to Blair was like Jenny learning that she would not be able to work at the gym, at least for the next six weeks. She had been very upset about that, since she felt that was God's main way of using her. Being out of commission was not easy for Jenny. Even when she was doing chemo, she only missed a few days of work here and there, and a one-week stretch when she had been hospitalized, but six whole weeks? That seemed like an eternity.

Ryan felt particularly thrilled by the food. He had wondered how much take out Jenny would put up with during her recovery. Now, it was no longer an issue.

The ladies decided to leave because even though Jenny looked better, she still was exceptionally wiped out. Before they left, they prayed for her, thanking God that she was still her, was going to be okay, and praising God repeatedly for their friendship and how God was changing each of them.

Jenny was reflecting on how much God had changed her heart in the last thirty-six hours. From being able to accept help, to allowing God to change her heart when it came to adoption, she knew from here on out life would be vastly different. She was learning that when it came to God and what He wanted for our lives; sometimes you had to close your eyes, jump in head first, and take a very literal leap of faith.

11

The next week passed quickly. The women were together often, as they were at Jenny's as much as possible, keeping her company and encouraging her. On Friday afternoon, Jenny finally got up the nerve to tell Monica what had happened. Monica, being such a grace-filled person, gave Jenny a caring hug and promised her that it was ok. Emotions like that are part of being human and we simply had to ask for forgiveness and move on. How did Monica always have such a simple answer, so filled with faith? "You are the biggest blessing, Mon." Monica blushed and looked away.

Then, Jenny, seeing her opportunity, began a playful ribbing, "So, speaking of big blessings, how the stud muffin? Did he give you the ring yet?" Oh, she never grew tired of picking on her sweet, easily embarrassed friend.

Monica replied, "He's great. We are great. And no, I don't have a ring yet. But, I can honestly say I want to be that man's wife so much it hurts sometimes. I know it has only been a few weeks, but that is all I need. And, Mandy just adores him. They have bonded instantly. And even Mom and Dad are thrilled." Suddenly Monica threw her hands up over her mouth and said, "Listen to me going on and on like a little school girl."

Jenny laughed loudly. Had her neck brace not been supporting her healing collar bone, it would have been one of those laughs where one throws their head backwards. "Monica, I love seeing you so happy. You deserve happiness, you and Mandy both."

Around three o'clock, Lizzy arrived to take over Jenny's care until Ryan arrived home. Monica had to rush home to meet Mandy to get her off the bus. She made it just in time, hopping out of the car and meeting Mandy at the end of the driveway. Mandy always loved checking the mail, and she excitedly pulled the stack of mail out of the mailbox.

Monica thumbed through the pile. Most of it was for her parents and would be set neatly on the island in the kitchen. There was a letter for Mandy from her pen pal in Spain. Monica loved that program and how it helped Mandy appreciate all kinds of people. There were some circular ads for the two biggest local grocery stores, and there, at the bottom of the pile was a letter that made her heart stop.

The handwriting was sloppy and hard to read. But, in the upper left hand corner was the name of the sender. It was from Deke from the Kentucky home he still owned. "Mandy, I know it's the beginning of the weekend, but can you please go do your homework right away? Mommy has something she needs to take care of."

"Sure, Mommy." How had she ended up with such a sweet girl, especially when her father had been so awful to both of them? Quickly, Monica did the math. It had been sixteen months since they had even heard from Deke by letter, longer since he had called Mandy. That had been two Christmases ago. Mandy sent letters to her Dad often, giving him promises of how Jesus loved him, and how she missed him. But not once since their divorce had Deke asked to see her. And Monica, hoping never to look into Deke's angry dark eyes again, had never pressed the issue. Sometimes an absent father could be a gift, especially if the man was cruel and abusive.

She was trying to open up the envelope, but her hands were shaking so bad that she could barely slip her finger in the small area unsealed at the top of the letter. She pulled it out and was both relieved and disheartened to see that the letter was addressed to her and not to Mandy. Mandy deserved a father who loved her, who desired to be part of her life. Monica often had blamed herself for choosing the wrong man to be with, but had made peace with how hard she had worked to make the dysfunctional marriage succeed. She had tried. She had been willing to forgive the other women and the abuse, but Deke has tossed her aside like a dirty towel. The pain had hurt so bad initially, but Monica could see how there was good in it as well. So many women stayed in dysfunction for years and years, and even if it was through abandonment, was rescued from that existence. Even though she was living with her parents, Monica had made a life for her and Mandy. They were happy, stable, and living a life that glorified God. It was okay. Yes, it was okay, until that very moment when Monica read that first line of the letter.

The group all sat there in disbelief. Monica stared at the letter in her hand, Dekes handwriting now smudged from her tear drops. Her hands were trembling and no one knew what to say. Silent tears fell from her eyes. Blair's mind twisted and turned, questioning how she could even care about the man after the years of torture she had endured, but seeing the heartache in her eyes, it was obvious that he would always have a special place in her heart.

The letter had gone on to explain how thankful Deke was that Monica had always been loving towards him, even when he had not deserved it. It also talked about how he had changed his life, and had been trying to live better. He asked if he could see Mandy. The thought of such an awful man being near the little girl made Blair bristle with anger. Then, the end of the letter came with a sad announcement. Deke had cancer. And according to his doctors he only had a few weeks left to live.

Everyone tried to think of what to say to Monica, or just even something to say out loud. The silence was the first time Blair ever remembered feeling awkward around these incredible women, and truth be told, she just wanted to run right out of that room. Yes, over the last few weeks, these women had taken her in, dove into an intense friendship with her, and made a lasting impact on not only herself, but her family. But, this was a whole new level of friendship. She had no idea how to walk through a trial like this with someone else.

Lizzy, being the fearful leader broke the intense pause in conversation. "Monica, I know this sounds trite, but it's true. God is working for your good here. His Word promises to grow us in trials and tribulations."

Monica looked Lizzy in the eye. What was usually a soft, warm, understanding face looked angry. "Lizzy, you have no idea what it is like to be me. How abandoned I feel by God right now. Just when things were looking up in my life, now I have to deal with this. My parents are threatening to throw me out if I let Deke see Mandy. Do you understand that? How could that possibly be what is best for me? To be homeless? To be alone? What if this messes up things with Jer? I have no idea what is best for my little girl. You have no idea. Your life is perfect from the inside out all the time."

Blair looked back and forth between Lizzy and Monica. Honestly, she was expecting Lizzy to retort back with a well-deserved backlash, but Lizzy said, "Monica, I know things look perfect to you. I'm sorry if my answer seemed insensitive, or if it came across as a platitude. I truly believe it with my whole heart. I know God will bring out the best in you through this." Lizzy then walked over to Monica and gave her a heartfelt hug, both women crying.

The other three women looked at one another, grateful that their friends would not continue in a heated argument. Kate surprised everybody and started praying out loud. Instead of an articulate prayer often prayed at Bible studies, Katie got down on her knees, lifted her hands to heaven and said in a wavering voice on the brink of tears, "God, we need you in our lives more than ever."

12

That evening, Lizzy was cleaning up after dinner. She and Brad had made a new dish that she had wanted to try to make for a while now. Spinach, tomatoes, chicken, with rich Italian cheese, all served over pasta. They ate at their little bistro table in the kitchen. A candle in the middle of the two of them, sweet smiles back and forth. And Brad had given his complete attention as Lizzy shared the events that had happened in the living room earlier that day. Brad had surprised her with a small portion of cheesecake that he ordered from a local Italian restaurant. They ate it slowly, enjoying each smooth, creamy bite, and then Brad took her hand and led her to her favorite spot in the whole house….her pink couch.

They sat down together. Lizzy nestled up in against Brad's right side. He gently turned her face towards his and gave her a sweet kiss. He then looked at her very seriously and said, "Lizzy, I think it's time that you share with the Bible study ladies who we are as a couple and what God has brought us through. It is time. It's obviously affecting your ministry with them."

Lizzy sighed and just shook her head no. However, she was gently rebutted with a very powerful claim from Brad. "Transparency is the key to ministry. I have been sharing with some men at work about what I've done and how God has redeemed me. I am so sorry every time I think about what I put you through, but it's time we put the shame behind us, and move forward. It's time we use our story as a ministry tool."

Lizzy groaned, knowing that he was right, though she had no idea how to tell the whole truth about who she was. Every time one of the girls mentioned how perfect things were in her marriage, she felt a pang of guilt. Yes, she and Brad loved each other. They prayed together. Brad had become an amazing spiritual leader in their home. But, what would they think about her when they found out the whole truth?

Still when she thought about that day, embarrassment would fill her cheeks. Every ounce of shame she felt from that day still could make her cry on a dime. What had she done to cause him to do it? How could she have stopped it? Eleven years later, and plenty of beautiful healing moments in their marriage, and she still was prone to self-doubt and blame.

The day she found out, she had an odd, unsettling feeling. Brad had been acting distant on one hand, but very attentive on the other hand. Now she looks back, and she can recognize what it was—guilt. She remembers seeing her husband's phone on the floor. It must have dropped out of his pocket. As she picked it up, she noticed a picture of another woman. The woman looked vaguely familiar. A thought passed through her mind at that moment, "No, Lizzy, you do not want to look any farther. Do not scroll through those photos. You know you do not want to see what is there." But, she hadn't listened, and still to this day the next few pictures of a scantily clad woman are engrained into her heart. They make her shudder, and cry, and weep. And she still struggles with emotions concerning the woman, who she now recognizes as Shelly, a supervisor at Brad's old job. Lizzy also flushes when she thinks about the rage she felt that night. No rage ever before that moment had ever seized her that way, and she doubts that she will ever feel like that again. Once the pictures had confirmed what Lizzy had hoped wasn't true, she stomped into the next room and asked him about the pictures. Brad had stood speechless in front of her. He couldn't even think of a word to say. Lizzy then began screaming at him. The hurt of the pictures and what they represented was so hard to swallow. She had always thought of their marriage as nearly picture perfect. Yes, they had their troubles, but what couple didn't?

To be so hot with rage, so ashamed and embarrassed, and to feel so worthless all in the same moment was one of the worst sensations of her life. However, she will never forget how even in that moment, she knew God's Spirit was working in her soul. She was going to love Brad through this. And she could not believe the words tumbling out of her lips, "If you think this is going to make me leave you, you are wrong. I will find a way to love you, love you all the way back to Jesus." And while the words were sweet when you think about them now, they were not sweetly spoken at that point in time. They were screamed in Brad's face, just as she smashed the phone against the wall. Lizzy had never yelled at her husband before. They had been married for twelve years, and while they had spats, and sometimes things had been heated, she had never yelled, let alone screamed in her husband's face. For the first time in her life, she actually felt like she could have hit someone. "How could you do this to me? To our family? What about the boys? Did you think about anyone besides youself?"

The next several weeks were hard for her to work through. She was just too ashamed to tell anyone. How could she ask her friends for help? She was planning to stay with Brad and she didn't want anyone to think less of him, or her, for that matter. She knew deep down in her heart he didn't mean to hurt her the way he had. Sin had gotten the best of him. God had been clear in showing her that while Brad's sin was tremendously hurtful, he still needed to be handled with grace. God often brought to Lizzy's mind all the little white lies she had told her whole life. And how some of those untruths still made her feel unworthy of God's love, or even Brad's love. She knew what it was like to sin habitually, and how one lie could lead to a bigger one. She imagined that this was the case with what happened with Brad. One compromise led to another. Every time she wanted to throw all his sin in his face, she would be reminded of her own sin and how she needed just as much grace from God and Brad as he needed.

She was also humbled by how much Brad had forgiven her over the years. There was a season early on in their marriage when Lizzy had been demanding and hard to please, placing unrealistic expectations on Brad. There had been seasons when she had spending problems, or anger issues. Brad had always forgiven her. Lizzy often debated within her mind if had caused Brad to cheat. What had she done to push him away? Was she at fault? Brad always assured her that the decisions he had made were more about his own sin than her, but they both agreed that Lizzy still expected an awful lot from her husband. Part of the pull for Brad to stray had been based on the constant adoration from his boss.

Brad never justified his sin with that information, but rather they used that to help them rebuild their marriage. Lizzy had become Brad's constant cheerleader. When she was feeling agitated with Brad, she would turn to God and ask Him to help her love Brad more. And Brad would openly share with Lizzy when he was feeling a little rundown from the world. They had become a team that worked together, instead of becoming obsessed with placing blame.

Still, it was awful, just miserable working through it all alone. A few people noticed that she hadn't been acting like her normal self, but Lizzy would just reply that life had been pretty tough lately. She felt inadequate because in her mind, if she had been good enough, Brad would have never wandered. He would have been satisfied with her and all she had to offer. Obviously, he hadn't been. That was the hardest thing to accept. Well, that was, until she went to counseling. The counseling session was humiliating. Admitting to someone else she was not sure if she would ever feel comfortable having physical relations with her husband again was painful to admit out loud. What was even more painful was the fact that the counselor suggested that sometimes in these situations, it was healthier for the couple to part ways, even if just for a couple weeks. Lizzy loved Brad so much. Despite the hurt, she could not imagine ever parting ways from him. She told the counselor that would *not* be happening, and she walked out of that office and never went back in.

For months, Lizzy, normally happy and joyful, just walked around, dull and lifeless. It felt as if there was a dark cloud over everything. As Lizzy remembered this time in her life, tears just fell. The girls needed to know her past. They needed to know that she and Brad were not perfect. But, most importantly they needed to know how God had changed her through this experience.

Another thought passed through her mind. About two weeks after walking out of the therapist's office, Lizzy knew that something had to be done about the darkness in her soul. She typed in the Google box, "What Bible passage helps when you need joy?" A blog came up that walked her through Psalm 51. To this day, Lizzy thinks about those scriptures on a regular basis. They tell us how God can wash us and make us whiter than snow. But, it also says how God desires for us to have a broken spirit. He wants us to turn our broken parts all over to Him and let him mold us together into something more beautiful, more creative, more unique, and even more purposeful.

That had happened in their marriage. Yes, they had traveled some hard roads right after the affair had been discovered. Brad, knowing in his heart what was right and honorable, quit his job. Thankfully, he found another one very quickly. He knew he had to get away from the woman who had captivated him enough to pull him away from his Lizzy. While his new job wasn't exactly his dream job, it paid well, and it had shown Lizzy that he was serious about repenting of his sin. Yes, Christmas and Valentine's Day had been very rough that year, trying to figure out who they were, and what they meant to each other. There were days where they would only talk business, and the thought of talking pleasure never even entered their mind. They went through the motions of being married, but behind those motions were the deep roots of commitment they did have for each other, for the Lord, and to somehow see this marriage still work out.

Lizzy kept praying that God would help her lose the bitter seed that had tried to wedge its way into her heart. And day by day, after the first two months, which were mostly just working through hurt, they softened towards one another. Brad had sought counseling too, and his had been much more effective, particularly dealing with his sin head-on. He even joined a men's accountability group at church and shared openly and honestly with an accountability partner. He continually made plans to devote himself more and more to God and Lizzy, and less to his sinful ways. As Brad surrendered wholeheartedly to Christ, a man emerged that Lizzy could not help but to fall deeper in love with.

Yes, yes, these girls needed to know what a difference God could make, even when dealing with the biggest sins imaginable. Even when working through big hurts. Lizzy knew that Brad had been right. It was time to come clean. It was time to let everyone see the marriage that she and Brad had for what it truly was, a redeemed, messy story, full of heartache, but brimming with hope.

13

Monica was so tired of recounting everything awful that had happened over the last two days. She knew, from Deke's letter that time was of the essence and she had to make decisions fast. Monica was ashamed of her outburst at Lizzy. She knew Lizzy really believed the word of God and trusted in Him wholeheartedly. Late Tuesday evening, after their Bible study, Lizzy had called and shared a surprising story with her about how God's word had carried her and Brad through an affair. Monica was shocked by the news, but amazed that faith in God's word had really restored their marriage. She also knew that her parents were trying to watch out for both her and Mandy. When Monica had showed her parent the letter, her dad became enraged in a way that Monica had never seen. "No! Absolutely not! That man can never be around my Mandy or my girl ever again. I *swear to you, Monica*, if you take that little girl anywhere near him, you are outta here. Gone! The choice is yours but you better make the right one."

Monica had never had a confrontation like this with her parents before, ever. Even in high school, during those quarrelsome years, she had always been obedient and a people pleaser. "Daddy, he's dying, *dying*. He *is* her father." And Monica started to cry. Embarrassed of her tears, of her frustration and anger at her father for being so narrow minded, she retreated to her small bedroom down the hall. She cried, prayed, and then sobbed some more. After about a half an hour, her sweet mother came knocking on the door.

"Monica, sweetie. Here I brought you some water and Tylenol. I know you will need it after the way you have been carrying on, dear." Monica nodded her head and swallowed the medicine quickly. She prayed it would do its job swiftly as her head was already pounding with a vengeance. "Sweetie, you need to understand that your dad is not being unreasonable here. Monica, you will never know how much it hurt us to know that man was hurting you. We felt like we failed you. You father sat in his chair, prayed for you every single night. While other men were watching football, he would watch the phone, praying you would call saying you needed us. Sometimes, he would get so angry with Deke, he would want to hurt him. Instead, we prayed for your safety." Monica nodded, understanding how hard it would be if someone was hurting Mandy. "Do you remember when you would call on Friday nights when Deke was out partying? We would always ask you to come home. You would say no, saying you had to work it out with him. We did our best to support you. But, now that you are free from him, we can't let you go back there."

"Mom, I have Jer now. I'm not ever going back to Deke." Monica's answer came quick, and it surprised her.

"Monica, I don't think you ever realized the hold that man had on you. He controlled you more than we realized, more than you will ever know."

"Mom, I got this."

"Just be careful, Mon. We love you so much, and our sweet Mandy." She began to cry thinking of the awful things that Mandy's young memory had hopefully erased about her abusive father. "And, Monica, I'm really not sure your dad will ever change his mind about this. Be forewarned." Monica nodded in agreement with her mother. Then her mom said something that Monica had only let herself think about once, in a passing thought. "Have you told Jer yet? What does he have to say about all of this?"

Monica knew that Jer needed to know. Here it was two days later, and Monica finally felt like she had enough courage to tell him. "Hey, Jer, it's Mon. Listen, I have something important I want to talk to you about. Will you meet me at the park this evening around 6:30?"

"Great! I can't wait to see you," Jer replied way too chipper for the news that Monica was going to deliver.

Dinner that night was full of highs and lows. Her parents were being very gentle with her, overcompensating for the fight they had before. Mandy, thankfully, was oblivious to everything going on around her. She chattered about the story she was writing about a kitten named Candy that loved to eat Skittles and then paints things with her paws. Then she told a story about her classmate Andy who stuffed fourteen tater tots in his mouth, and then went home early when he threw up. She laughed as recounted a tale about gym class and how they had played with the parachute that day. She said her favorite part was going underneath the huge colorful semicircle and feeling like you were lost in a rainbow, such happy stories for a little girl that was unknowingly surrounded by conflict.

As Monica finished scraping the little bits of spaghetti left on plates into the garbage and filling the dishwasher, she asked God to give her the right way to tell Jer about the letter. She also prayed for a favorable response from him. She gave Mandy a kiss and told her to wash up and get to bed around eight. She promised Mandy good night snuggles, even if she was fast asleep when her Momma got home. Monica walked out the door, breathing in the fall air. It was crisp and cool, but not cold, good hoodie weather. She walked quickly, hurrying to get there. As she traveled she saw so many happy people. It seemed unfair that everyone else seemed to be having a carefree night, and the weight of the world, at least her and Mandy's world, was resting on her shoulders.

She found the bench they had agreed to meet on. It stood out from all the other benches because someone had spray painted it with orange graffiti that said, "Jesus Saves." Monica always felt uneasy about graffiti with a Christian message. She wondered to herself what Jesus would think about it. Maybe He would like the publicity. It was an important message. But, Monica reasoned, the Bible said they will know we are Christians by our love, and not by our graffiti. She went back and forth in a pretend debate in her mind to pass the time by while she waited for Jer.

In just a few minutes, he was there. He was as handsome as ever, even though he wore workout pants and a ragged hoodie from his college years. As they hugged, Monica took a deep breath. "Ahhh, I love the way he smells," she thought. It made her stomach a little flip floppy and she smiled at him, despite the news she was bearing.

"Jer, do you mind praying for us before I tell you what I need to tell you?""Are you okay? Are you hurt, Monica?"

"It's going to be okay, but I need God to help me be brave and tell you about something that has come up this week."

Jer prayed a prayer asking for God to encourage Monica. He also asked for a dose of understanding for himself. God must have heard that prayer because Jer proved himself to be quite the man by his response. "Monica, what others may see as you letting people get away with, I see as you demonstrating mercy. You are a forgiving person. You are humble. You meet people where they are at. I want to support you any way I can in being the person God called you to be. Does Deke know about me?"

"No, he hasn't spoken to us in two years."

"Well, just for safety reasons, would you be okay with me going with you when you take Mandy? Or is that overstepping what you want from me right now?"

"Jer, I can't think of a better response that I would want from you."

They looked intently into each other's eyes, realizing that this moment would be locked in their minds as a defining moment of their relationship. They were figuring out how to be exactly who they each needed the other to be. After a couple nervous glances, and flushed faces, Monica offered the letter over to Jer, who read it quickly.

"He sounds sincere Monica. He just wants to say good-bye. Do you want to make plans to drive up there on Saturday?"

She nodded and agreed that they would make the seven-hour trip.

"Oh no!" Monica exclaimed suddenly.

"What's wrong, hon?" Jer questioned.

"My dad, what about my dad?"

Jer assured her that he would talk to her dad. He had a feeling that once Monica's dad had a fresh perspective on her calling and life, and the fact that she was going with male protection, maybe his perspective would change.

Jer walked her home since it was getting dark out. He even decided to talk to her dad that night. Sure enough, he had her father pegged. He was so worried about her safety, and he awkwardly hugged Jer and told him how thankful he was to have him in their life.

Monica cuddled in next to Mandy. As suspected, the precious little blessing was fast asleep. Monica sniffed the little girl's clean curls of hair, smelling the strawberry scented shampoo mixing with the watermelon bubble bath that Mandy always used. This little girl was the center of her heart. While many of the week's decisions had been made, and several conflicts resolved, there was one remaining hurdle to jump, telling Mandy.

14

Blair was super excited to have a day all to herself. She and Samuel had been finding their groove at the new church, meeting new people, and had actually found themselves quite busy lately. They had gone over to a couple's house for dinner one night, they had gone to Bible study another evening, and Blair and the kids had gone to Jenny's after school several times to help out. Jenny was bouncing back quickly, so she decided to do a few hours on her own today, which had given Blair the day off. She decided right away that today was going to be a splurge-on-me kind of day. She made a last minute appointment for a haircut, and had planned on getting a massage after that. She remembered her one friend in their old town telling her about a massage that had warm rocks they put on your back. Since the weather was turning colder and her stress level had risen from their busier schedule, she thought that sounded like a great plan. First, she thought she would head to the local coffee shop. They had this amazing chocolate Danish there. She had eyed it up before, but had never indulged. Today was the day, a day all about her. Every single bite was perfect, and she was sad when the last morsel was consumed.

She arrived at the salon and got seated in the reclining chair in front of the sink. Was there anything better than having someone else scrub your scalp? Blair wondered if they took lessons on that in beauty school. As her scalp tingled from the repetitive motion of the beautician's nails, she heard her phone ring. She had the lady stop for just a moment so she could check the number that was dialing in. When Blair saw that it was the school calling, she felt a surge of panic ripple through her.

"Hello?" she said as soon as she flipped open her old cell phone.

"Hello is this Ava's mother?"

"Yes, this is Blair? How can I help you?"

I have your daughter here in the nurse's office. She is vomiting and has a fever. Are you able to come get her?"

"Yes, I'll be there in about twenty minutes."

Blair looked at the hairdresser with sad eyes. "I'm sorry. Can you rinse me? My daughter is sick."

The woman was obviously annoyed with Blair and responded with a gruff, "You know, you still have to pay for the shampoo." It took everything she had in her not to respond with a bad attitude right back to the lady. Actually, Blair was kind of surprised at the fact that she hadn't responded back the way she felt the lady deserved. She walked up to the counter with hair that was soaked and paid the five dollars for her hair wash. Feeling a prompt from what Blair assumed was the Holy Spirit, she actually tipped the lady too. Then, she left quickly to go get Ava.

The entire drive to the school, Blair struggled with a couple of emotions. Truly, she was concerned about Ava, but she felt so disheartened. She just needed a day to take care of herself. Was it so much to get her hot stone massage and a haircut? For crying out loud, she only scheduled a haircut once a year anyway.

Blair finally admitted to herself that she was a little ticked off. She wanted time for herself. She was always being pulled in one direction or another by everyone else. The first day in months she had taken a time out, and now she was reporting for duty, five and a half hours early, and with hair that was making her t-shirt wet.

The safety procedures at this school were very rigid. And it was even tougher for her because the school staff didn't know her. She was asked for her ID, and Blair realized that she had not brought it with her, so she had to walk back out to the car and dig around the glove compartment to find her wallet. Blair's frustration was mounting with each hurdle she had to jump over. It was all so annoying. Finally, she retrieved the ID and was granted access to the nurse's office.

Ava did look very pale, and her fever felt very high. The nurse said it was 103.5. Now that a parent was present, the nurse was able to give Ava some fever reducer. Ava swallowed the medicine, and they signed out of the office and got into the car and headed home. It was only a short drive from the school to her house. As they had turned into the driveway, her phone rang again.

"Are ya kidding me?" Blair said out loud as she saw the school's number again. Now Franklin was there, with the same symptoms. "Can you please just call Charlie to the office too? I may as well save myself the drive." So, while leaving Ava in the car, Blair hopped out, making sure to have her ID with her this time, and went in the school to pick up the boys. Poor Franklin looked awful, but Charlie, he looked furious.

"Mom! I can't leave school! I have a football game after school today."

"Charlie, I'm not coming back to the school when you get sick. Your siblings are all sick. Everyone needs to come home and rest. I'm not having the best day. *Please*, just listen to me and do what you are told."

"Mom, the football game. I'm not sick. I need to go to the football game."

Blair debated. He did look fine. And he was a part of the team. "Fine, stay and go. Dad will come to your game tonight. K? Love you, honey." She hugged him good-bye and her and a greenish looking Franklin walked out of the school.

She ran into the local store and got some Gatorade and ginger ale and then she took the kids home and got them each tucked into their bed with buckets on the floor next to them. She realized the nurse had never given Franklin any fever reducer, so she gave him the medicine. For the next hour, she went between rooms, dampening washcloths with cold water, finding the right amount of blankets to cover each kid with, and praying for each of them. It was exhausting. Blair decided the only thing worse than one kid sick, was two. She nodded in agreement with herself and chuckled because sometimes the truth is funny.

Ava fell asleep quickly, probably thanks to the medicine, and Franklin had fallen asleep after about forty minutes of getting comfortable, throwing up twice, and a dozen "Mommy, I need this and I need that" statements. Finally, Blair washed her hands, popped some vitamin C tablets and sat down with a magazine and a cup of tea. She had no sooner opened her magazine to the table of contents when the phone rang once again. "You *have* to be kidding me." She didn't even say hello when she saw the phone number. "Let me guess. I need to come get Charlie now too."

Of course she did. And even though her kids could probably stay by themselves for the half an hour needed to drive to the school, sign Charlie out, and come back home, Blair was not sure if she felt safe leaving the kiddos. So, she had to do what she had to do. She woke both sick, sleeping kids up, to pick up their stubborn, sick brother.

After Charlie was in the car, all three kids took on a new level of crankiness that Blair had not seen since the early years when they would miss a naptime. Everyone was short tempered and grumpy with one another. At one point, Charlie called Franklin a dummy, and Blair lost it. She turned around, looked all three of them in the eye, all at once, like only a Mom can and began to scream at them. "Listen here, all three of you. I've had *enough*. This was supposed to be mom's relaxing day. I was supposed to have a day alone to do whatever I wanted and instead I've been to the school three different times, picking up three different kids. Enough. Not another word. I'm so frustrated I could scream."

Franklin, being so sensitive, began to cry. And Charlie, being so irritable about missing his football game told Franklin that crying was wussy and he needed to stop being so stupid. At that point, Blair snapped. She turned around and slapped Charlie on his cheek. "I told you not another word." Stunned, with tears in his eyes, Charlie didn't dare speak again. No one did. And they rode home in the most awkward silence their family had ever experienced.

The silence continued as each kid filed out of the car, into the house, and straight into his or her bed. Blair could not believe she had slapped Charlie. She had never, ever hit a child out of frustration before. She knew she had apologizing to do. She just had no idea how to go about it.

15

"Ryan, I would like to talk to you." It had been a couple weeks since her accident. Jenny was feeling much better and the pain was decreasing each day. Blair normally spent a couple hours with Jenny most days after school got out, but today, Jenny wanted to be on her own. She cooked one of the freezer meals from Blair tonight, and made pudding for dessert, even if she had to use her kitchen aid mixer to do the stirring for her. She lit the taper candles that always stood proud and unburned on their dining room table and made their two spots beautiful by using their prettiest placemats, cloth napkins and fancy napkin holders. By the time she was done, it looked like a five star restaurant, even if it was just homemade macaroni and cheese from the freezer and boxed pudding.

Looking at Ryan, she reached over and held his hand, very gingerly with her right hand. Sometimes it still hurt if she moved too fast.

"Ryan, every time I feel pain left over from my accident, it reminds me of how terrible I was to you and how resistant I was to God. My selfishness took over, and that led me to act out in anger. My anger not only put my own life at risk, but also risked the life of the man who I pulled out in front of, even if unintentionally. I'm so ashamed of the mistakes I've made. I've been talking to God about forgiving me, and I feel he has, but…"

Ryan held her hand up to keep her from talking anymore. He

didn't want guilt to be hanging over her head any longer. "You are forgiven and loved, sweetie, by both of us."

She had expected Ryan to say something like that. She was grateful for the kind of man he was. A godly man who extended a lot of grace to people, but he gave Jenny more grace than anyone could ever ask for.

"Ryan, there's one thing you are forgetting. When we ask for forgiveness, we are to repent. Repenting means me turning from anger and selfishness. And the best way I can think to do that is to open my heart to a child."

"Jenny, you don't have to do this to prove anything to me. I know you love God. I know you want to serve Him. You don't have to prove anything to me."

"Hon, I'm not trying to prove anything. I'm just trying to be obedient to the way God has changed my heart."

She went on to explain how she had been thinking about the verse they had studied last week in Bible Study. "Love must be sincere. Hate what is evil and cling to what is good. I read that verse a hundred times this week. What is evil is how children are abused, abandoned, and tossed away. What is evil is selfishness. What is good? Sincere love. I want to cling to what is good. And loving a child that needs us would be amazing."

Ryan teared up as he realized that only God could have changed Jenny's heart about this. Ryan had not said another word to her about it after she had so blatantly told him how she felt about it the night before the accident. Here God had worked on her heart all on His own. Then Jenny told about a dream she had the night before.

"I was holding her. She was blonde. Not a normal blonde, but angelically blonde. Like her head was shining. And she was nestled against me and she called me Mama. I want it, Ryan. I never knew I did, but I do."

"So you are telling me you actually want this? For sure?"

"God has definitely put a desire in me. I know it is a fast change, but God is big enough to handle fast changes. And this has been the only time in my life that I've ever just laid around and thought. Even when I was doing chemo, I was always chatting with people at the cancer center. Here, I spent so much time just thinking. And thinking leads to praying. And apparently praying leads to babies." Jenny smiled brightly at him and they hugged each other.

"So, should I throw this macaroni in the microwave and heat it back up?" Ryan asked?

"No, let me do it. I'm cooking tonight, remember?" Jenny said with a lighthearted sound in her voice that hadn't been there for weeks.

While she was heating up the plates, Ryan walked over to the calendar, grabbed a red sharpie and drew a heart over that particular Friday. It was a day that he would cherish forever.

16

Lately, Kate felt a guilty about not seeing her friends very much. She had spent a lot of time with Phil and the boys. The Bible study that he was attending really encouraged a lot of family bonding, spending time together, praying together, playing games together, just being in each other's presence. It was difficult for Kate to admit that they really had never done much of it as a family. But, she thought that the leader of the Bible study may have been on to something. The kids were behaving more than they had ever before. One of the family points was to have a family meeting and to review expectations and consequences. The kids, especially Jeff, loved having everything lined out for him. "So you are saying if I yell at you or Dad, I get a time-out? Well, I guess I better quit yellin'!"

Structure seemed to be the key to ironing out some of the issues in their family. It was not perfect, but the improvements were dramatic and their family was so different over the last couple weeks.

Still, Kate felt a little guilty because Jenny had been in the wreck. While Kate had been there that day and an afternoon or two with Jenny during recovery, the only thing she had really done consistently is to pray. But, she reminded herself that her family was her primary calling in life. While her friends were very important, her two little boys were a specific task, given directly to her from the Lord. Kate was working on balancing false guilt with personal responsibility. It was a difficult task.

She decided to call Jenny and check on her. But, first, she would make herself a cup of coffee. As Kate scanned the cupboard she saw a little red container that she bought at the store a few weeks ago and never made. It was an English Toffee cappuccino mix. Not exactly coffee, but it sounded delightful. So, she put the hot water on the stove and got down her biggest, prettiest mug. The mug held at least what two normal cups would and on the side it had a beautiful sketch of a sailboat. Amazing grace had been etched on the side. She'll never forget when her friend, Misty, had given it to her as a little celebration when Kate told her about deciding to follow Jesus. Misty had then shared how she had prayed for years for Kate and Phil and how happy it made her to know that not only had God answered her prayers, but that Kate was going to experience life to the fullest. Here it was two years later and Kate really was starting to get a glimpse of what life could be when following Jesus. It excited her and made the words, amazing grace, come alive even more to her.

Kate scooped the mix into the cup. She poured the hot water in and mixed it with a little whisk. She then added some half and half, a big dollop of cool whip, and just to make it like a coffee shop, she drizzled it with some caramel ice cream topping. It was going to be a great cup of coffee while she talked on the phone with a wonderful friend. Kate tried to decide if she had ever felt so blessed in her life. Maybe felt blessed wasn't the right word. Kate tried to think of how to phrase it. Then she wrote down on the little notepad by the phone, "Have I ever recognized so many blessings in my life before?"

With that thought, she dialed the familiar numbers of Jenny's home phone number. When Jenny answered, she sounded different than normal. Even though Jenny had a naturally vibrant voice, she sounded absolutely radiant today.

"What's up with you, girl? You sound like you are about ready to burst!" Kate inquired.

"I am, Kate! I am!"

"Tell me what in the world is going on," Kate begged.

"I'll tell you on Tuesday." Jenny teased.

"C'mon, tell me, puhlease!" Kate laughed at how much like a kid she sounded. Jenny did too.

"Listen to you whining. I guess I better figure out how to deal with whining if I'm gonna be a mom!"

Kate squealed "*What*! I thought that wasn't possible."

Jenny smiled and reflectively said, "Anything is possible with God. We are meeting with a social worker on Monday to start filling out paperwork to adopt a baby, a child. We don't know. We just want God to use us however he sees fit."

"Oh, Jenny, this is amazing! How? When? What?" They both giggled, and then they dreamed about what the future may hold for Jenny and Ryan.

The cup of coffee did taste great that morning. But nothing tasted as great as knowing that she and her friends were seeking the will of God in their lives.

17

It was 4:00 a.m. on Saturday morning. It seemed ridiculous to be up that early. Mandy, who was usually quite compliant with most matters, was very outspoken about how she had not planned on being up that early either. Thankfully, Jer was a very patient man, and he had brought a nice cup of coffee and a cup of hot chocolate to lure them out of bed and onto the road. They had many miles to cover that day, and a big daunting visit in front of them.

As Mandy drank her hot chocolate, it did not take long for her to perk up and settle into her normal disposition. She enjoyed being around Jer and her mom. She told her mom two nights ago, "Momma, I love how your face smiles when Jer is around. You look like a light bulb all happy and glowy." Hearing Mandy gush about Jer made her wish more and more each day that there could be a happily ever after waiting for them right around the corner.

They drove out of town and then got on the interstate and headed north. Thanks to Jer's GPS, the trip was pretty mindless driving, just following the instructions of the GPS voice. It was nice to have not to worry about navigation, and instead they could just chat.

It was getting closer to the later part of October. The leaves were changed and brilliant. As the sun rose the glow radiating from the trees put all three travelers in awe. Jer asked Mandy what her favorite part of nature was. "I like how God makes things shiny with the sun." The adults nodded their head. What a beautiful answer.

They oohhed and ahhed over the view as they drove north, with the Great Smoky Mountains over to their east. They asked hundreds of questions during their drive. They learned about how Jer loved playing board games, but hated it when his younger brother beat him. They learned how Monica loved listening to classical music and sip tea when life felt out of control. But the most surprising thing that kept coming up was how much Mandy wanted them to be a family.

When Mandy brought up family a fourth time, Monica thought it was only appropriate to start the final preparations of seeing her biological father.

"Mandy, do you remember who we are going to visit?"

"My daddy named Deke."

"That's right, honey. Do you remember why we are going to go see him?"

"My daddy named Deke is sick. He wants to see me. He might die. I remember he was a mean man, Momma. But, I know that if I talk about Jesus he may turn into a nice man. Is that right, Mom? Can I make Daddy Deke a nice man?"

Monica took a deep breath. She looked at Jer with tears in her eyes.

Jer decided to help Monica out and answer the best he could. "Mandy, sweetie, we can't make someone a nice man just by talking about Jesus. Jesus has to change someone's heart. Your Daddy Deke has a lot of hurt in his heart. He hurt you and your momma because of all the pain in his own heart. The only thing we can do is pray that Jesus makes your Daddy Deke's heart open to God. "

Jer wasn't sure if that was the best answer in the world, but it was his best answer and it really seemed to appease Mandy at least.

Mandy said, "I will pray. I pray that Daddy Deke already asked Jesus to change his heart and that when we see him today he's a nice man. Wouldn't that be incredible?"

Monica responded very cautiously, "Mandy, God can work miracles, he definitely can. But he doesn't force someone to change, they have to be ready."

"Momma, don't you think it shows he's ready since he asked to see me?"

Monica didn't know how to tell her baby girl that he was just a dying man trying to gain some peace. Throughout the whole conversation, she just kept thanking God that Jer was there.

"Momma, what *do* you think?"

"Sweetie, I think we should just wait and see. Let's just wait and see."

"K, Momma."

A moment passed and the mood was solemn in the car.

"Momma, I love you. Jer, I wish you were my daddy. I wish that we weren't driving so far to see my Daddy Deke who might be mean to Mommy or me."

Jer looked over at Monica. She was crying the silent tears that moms figured out how to cry in the front seat of cars. The kind that moms learned how to cry when their husbands hit them, abandoned them, the tears that moms knew how to cry when life was so tough, but they just wanted their kids to be happy. She just let the tears flow.

Jer didn't know how to respond. So, he just drove, thankful that his GPS was alerting him of an interstate change two miles up ahead and that they were now halfway there.

Lizzy loved Saturdays—sleeping in. Pajamas, reading on her pretty pink couch while sipping hot cocoa. Since the October cool had come, she enjoyed baking again. The smell of banana bread wafted throughout her home. She felt so safe and secure here. She spent some time reading her Bible that morning and then prayed for each of her friends from Bible study. She especially prayed for Monica as they were traveling on their journey to see Deke. How brave she was. Monica was amazing at living out the "Love must be sincere" scenario. She was blessed to have such godly women to share her life with. She prayed for Jenny as she continued to recover. She had noticed yesterday on the phone how happy Jenny had sounded. It caught Lizzy off guard. She was so relieved to hear her friend sounding bubbly again, maybe even bubblier than normal. She wondered what the change could have been. She lifted up Kate, as well, asking God to keep working in their marriage. She was excited for them as their weekend away had been everything they seemed to need. The boys had enjoyed a special time with her and Brad. They played touch football, monopoly, and baked cookies. It had warmed Lizzy and Brad to have two young boys around again. And she knew the weekend had been a firm foundation for the spiritual changes that had been coming about in Kate and Phil. And then, there was Blair, her newest friend. It was a joy watching Blair learn about how she could serve the Lord just by being herself! Just watching the way she was learning was so encouraging and Lizzy felt a little nostalgic thinking about when she first started following the Lord and how exciting it seemed every single day. Lizzy sighed a big heavy sigh and prayed, "God, I want you to please work through me and with me to help me find that girl buried under routine and age. I want to be like Blair, rediscovering who you made me to be and what you want me to do."

It shook Lizzy up as she realized how much of her life had turned into routine. She did the same things over and over. Volunteer at the nursing home, decorate the church, cook dinner for Brad, plan the Bible study, maybe have someone over for dinner every now and then, then start the routine over again. She understood that not every time in life would be a mountain top, but she started to wonder to herself if she may be settling. She had been following the Lord for a long time. She loved hosting and teaching the Bible study, but she had even been leading that for several years. It wasn't really guilt that was stirring up inside her, but maybe a feeling of wanting something more. "God, help me find whatever I need from you to fill this void I'm feeling right now."

The emotions were starting to get to her and she felt she needed a little distraction, so she went to her tote bag and pulled out a book she had signed out from the library. The book was about a missionary in Tibet. It started out with a story about a spiritual attack that had left them terrified, ready to throw in the towel and resume a comfortable life in the United States. The missionary had actually ordered a plane ticket back home, when she had opened her Bible and read a verse. Ironically enough, it was the same verse that Lizzy was going to prepare for the Bible study lesson this week. It was from Romans 12:13. "Never be lacking in zeal, but keep your spiritual fervor, serving the Lord"

Lizzy just started crying, right there, on her comfy couch, in the middle of her beautiful living room, in her stately home, on the good side of town. She realized that truly was what was missing in her life was spiritual fervor. She decided that for her sake and the sake of the people God had entrusted her with leading that she would dig up some information on what it meant to have spiritual fervor.

18

It had been a full day since the slapping incident in the car. Blair had consumed herself with making sure each and every kid was well tended to physically as they recovered from the flu, but she still had not found the right way to apologize to her kiddos, especially to poor Charlie, who she had hit. She had talked to Samuel, who brushed it off saying, "Oh, that kind of thing happens sometimes sweetie. I'm sure the kids will forget about in no time." He was probably right, but still the general feeling in the home was off with this awful event still unresolved between them all.

The kids were all feeling better. No one had thrown up in over twelve hours and the fevers had gone from blazing to mild. Small doses of ginger ale, Gatorade, and saltines were dosed out on a two-hour schedule. When it came time for the noon serving of the sick kid delicacies, she decided to own up to the kids. It was not the ideal way for her to spend her Saturday afternoon. However, she decided that it was what was right.

"Kids, Sammy, please come here. I'm in the dining room."

In an effort to make the fare more palatable, she set the table with their finest china and poured ginger ale into their wine goblets. Just for good measure, she had lit two candles. The dining room never got much sun on that side of the house, so it was dim in the room, even at noon, and the setting looked warm and welcoming. She hoped it conveyed an atmosphere of apology.

As her family piled in, she had to do her best to hold back her tears. They were all so special. This was the family that God had given her. And she had such a bad attitude about taking care of them yesterday. Bible study phrases were just rolling through her mind: honor one another above yourselves, sober judgment, Love must be sincere.

"So, we are about to have a family meeting," Blair said with authority, even though she still had tears sitting in her eyes."

Franklin immediately began to cry. "I do not want to move again. I just made friends here. I love my room. *No!*"

"Franklin, we are not moving, bud. Why do you think that?" Samuel was trying to calm the emotional little boy before things got out of hand.

"Our last meeting like this, we moved to Tennessee. I finally am not missing North Carolina as much."

Everyone chuckled as they realized that their littlest member had a point. The last family meeting was the announcement that they would move to Tennessee. After assuring Franklin that an announcement of moving was not on today's agenda, Blair stated the real point of the meeting.

"Today, Mommy wants to apologize." Blair took a deep breath and asked her family to hear her out before they said anything else. "Yesterday I had planned a day all to myself. I was looking forward to relaxing and taking a time out. Mommies really can get their heart set on days like that sometimes." She then explained about the ID, and how frustrating it was to have to wake Ava and Franklin up, and how frustrated she had been when Charlie had refused to come home with her in the first place. "But, guys, here's the thing. According to the world, my behaviors may have even been justifiable. But, I'm learning that the world's standards are not what I want to live by. I want to live by God's standards. And if I'm using God's word as a measuring stick, I really fell short yesterday."

She looked right at Charlie. Her voice was shaking as she said, "Charlie, I'm so sorry I hit you yesterday. You should have never called your brother stupid, but in the same way, I should have never, ever hit you like that." Blair walked over and hugged him and he promised over and over that he forgave her.

"Mom, I should have just listened to you. I was being stubborn. And Franklin, I'm sorry, bud. You're not stupid. You are a great brother." Franklin flashed a smile at his brother and gave him a thumbs up sign.

Then she apologized to her entire family. "Sometimes, it's really easy to want things my way. Taking care of all of you is an honor. I'm going to work on trying to remember that." The rest of the meeting went very well. Apologies were made, forgiveness offered, and a more solid family connection was established. Blair couldn't believe how much better she felt apologizing to her kids. They decided since everyone was up and moving to play Uno. So right there with their fancy dishes, pretty table cloth, and candles they played Uno. As was almost always the case, Charlie won. The other kids had adapted to Charlie winning everything, but today, just because they were sick and bored, Ava demanded a rematch. This time, Blair won, which rarely happened. They all cheered for Blair, and while she was happy she finally won a family game, she felt more like she had won because of the miracle that was happening in her family as she grew and tried to follow God's word.

19

Monica's eyes were glued to the GPS screen. The mile countdown was starting to scare her. Forty miles left, turned into thirty in what felt like a minute, even though Jer was not speeding. Just a little over a half an hour, and she would have to face the one man who had caused her more pain, both physically and emotionally, than anyone else in the world. She closed her eyes and talked to Jesus about what would be happening. She prayed for Mandy's protection. She didn't want Mandy to ever hurt the way she had hurt when it came to Deke. She prayed for her heart. She talked to God about how Jer had just started to make her heart fully happy again, and now she had to face the man who had made her protect herself from hurt for years. "God, please help me to be kind to him. I know he doesn't deserve it. I know so many people think I shouldn't even be visiting him. But, God, this is what you want me to do. I know it. I want to extend your grace and your forgiveness, just like you show me all the time. God, I keep thinking about all those Bible verses, how to apply them to this situation, and all of them point to me being on this road right now, facing this man, being kind to him, even though he was unkind to me."

As she was finishing up her prayer, Jer reached over and held her hand. They had never held hands before. Jer was very careful about being pure physically, so they didn't even give themselves a chance to progress into the physical realm of a relationship. It seemed odd to

Monica, but she had grown accustomed to getting to know the man without physical contact. He carefully rubbed his thumb over her hand and whispered, "It's going to be okay. God's got this."

"Hey, I say that all the time," Monica responded sweetly.

Jer just smiled at her, thankful for this car ride. "Only eleven more miles to go."

They looked back at Mandy, who had fallen fast asleep. Her head was leaned against the window. Her curly blonde hair was making its way out of the French braid and was wispy. While it looked a little messy, it made cute little Mandy look even sweeter.

They got off the interstate with six miles to go. The GPS wasn't really needed at this point. They were headed to Monica's former mother-in-law's house. Her name was Sandy. The one thing about being married to Deke that Monica missed was Sandy. Sandy was the sweetest lady. Often times, both in marriage, and in divorce, Monica wondered how a delightful lady like Sandy could produce a man who was sometimes as monster-like as Deke was. It baffled her. Sandy's home was a small house. She was bordering on poverty ever since Monica had met her, but her modest house was always as neat as a pin. Even though she lived on wages from working as a cashier at the Salvation Army store, she was the most generous woman Monica had ever met. She remembered when Mandy was born how many clothes Sandy had bought them. And how she always compensated for Deke and Monica when Deke had spent all their money on booze, and they had no money for diapers or formula. Sandy had always been happy to help. She loved her son, and she loved Monica and Mandy. As she relived the pain of losing her mother-in-law, she felt badly. While Deke had been awful about sending cards or phone calls, Sandy had always sent presents to Mandy, had called her at least twice a month, and faithfully sent a letter that was penned after Sunday morning worship service every week. She really did miss Sandy in her life, and as much as the thought of seeing Deke scared her, she couldn't wait to see Sandy.

Deke had been staying with his mom for the last month. He had been so ill that he could no longer live on his own. Monica had called Sandy and arranged for them to arrive around noon. Sandy was excited to make lunch for them. As they made the last two turns of the long trip, the slowing car speed helped nudge Mandy out of her rest. "Mandy, we are almost there. We are almost at Gramma Sandy's."

"Mmmm, k, Momma."

They pulled into the familiar driveway. Monica felt like she was going to be sick. Upon arrival, they saw Sandy sitting on the rocking chair on the front porch. Sandy looked like she had aged forty years since Monica had last seen her. And Monica noticed right away that something was wrong. Sandy was crying. She looked forlorn. "Guys, can you stay in the car for just a minute?"

Monica slowly got out of the car and walked up to the porch. Sandy tried to muster a smile, but she looked down and shook her head. "Honey, he's gone. He died about eight this morning."

Monica just stood there speechless. How was she going to tell Mandy? Why had God brought them all the way up here for nothing? She walked over and hugged this woman, the only woman in the world who mourned her failed marriage as much as she did, even if for other reasons. "Oh, Sandy, sweet Sandy, I'm so sorry." Sandy tried to stand up, but she couldn't. She was too weak from grief. So, Monica did the only thing she could. She sat down, right in front of the rocking chair, and put her head in Sandy's lap. It was the same way they had sat the night Deke had abandoned his family. The women cried together. Jer, by observation put the pieces together, and gently told Mandy that her Gramma looked very sad and may need some extra hugs.

"Mandy, do you want to go love your Grammy? I think she may need you."

"Oh, yes! I love her. She sends me pretty Barbies and calls me honey girl in her letters." Mandy walked up to her Gramma's lap, and the three of them huddled there together mourning the loss of a man who had changed their lives, maybe not for the better, but he was truly a part of who they were, and now he was gone. Jer, being the gentleman he was, gave them time to sit there together, and he just prayed for them, remaining in the driver seat, with tears falling down his face for the two ladies he had come to love over the last few weeks.

Monica sat there for a long time, praying, sometimes silently, sometimes out loud. Mandy sat cuddled in her Grandma Sandy's lap. It had been so long since they had seen one another. Despite the distance between them, Sandy had always done whatever she could to keep in touch with Mandy, and Monica knew that Sandy being apart from Mandy was so painful for the woman. However, Sandy understood the pain that Monica had gone through and how it was vital during that time to keep their distance from Deke.

Monica realized that Jer was still sitting in the car. She opened her eyes, and wiped the tears so she could look over at him. There he sat, wiping his own eyes. It was at that point that Monica wondered how Sandy would feel about Jer. She only had thought about how safe it would make her feel to have him with her, but she had never considered how Sandy would feel. She felt remorseful for not being thoughtful about it before.

She cleared her throat and Sandy's eyes met hers. Sandy looked over at the car and saw Jer sitting there. "Who's da fella?" she asked. There was not a lot of emotion in her voice compared to the last sentences she spoke, so Monica couldn't exactly decide if Jer being there was a good thing or a bad thing.

Mandy smiled with pride as she said, "That's my Jer. Well, he's Momma's friend, but, he's mine too. He drove us here today so Mommy wouldn't be worried so much. Gramma, I think he's so nice. I think you will like him too." Sandy smiled at her granddaughter. She touched her golden braid and hugged her tight.

"Oh Mandy, you are such a sweet girl, just like your momma. You deserve to be happy." Looking at Monica she said quietly, "You do too, dear. I'm just sorry Deke stole so many years of happiness away from you." Monica started crying deep, throaty sobs as she realized the truth of what Sandy said. Sandy held her hand and promised her it was ok. In fact, Sandy was the one who finally waved Jer out of the car, even if it was after an awkwardly long time.

He came over, and hugged Sandy as if it was the most natural thing to hug your girlfriend's former mother-in-law. Sandy smiled at him, even though there was so much sadness in her smile. Her sweet nature shined through as she said, "Hello there. Jer is it? My girl, Mandy, here tells me that you are a sweet man. You are especially sweet to drive my girls up here today."

Mandy, only sort of grasping what had happened that day, went over and hugged Jer tightly. He picked her up and let her cuddle her head on his shoulder. He rubbed his cleanly shaven face against her soft cheek, which was warm from sleeping in the car and crying with her momma and gramma. Overcome with gratefulness and a protective feeling for this little girl, he just wanted to be everything to her that her now late father couldn't be.

20

Jenny was busy fixing up their house. By nature, she and Ryan were very neat people, so it wasn't like the house was out of sorts or anything. After all, it was just the two of them. However, she felt like the house seemed a little too pristine. She wanted the social worker to walk into their house and feel like a kid could be a kid here. Jenny's mom, while a very tidy person, was awesome at letting kids just be kids. She remembered how when she was little her mom would put a big pile of shaving cream on the table and tell them to have fun. They made mud pies and were never scolded for playing in the dirt like some of the neighbor kids were. Her momma always said she preferred muddy kids to boring kids. Jenny loved that about her mom and now that she was pursuing motherhood she wanted to make sure that she picked all the things out that she loved about her mom and share them with her own children.

Jenny got out the small box of toys she stored in the closet for when friends' kids came over. She pulled them out and put them in a cute wicker basket on the bottom of the bookshelf. She walked around filling all the empty outlets with outlet plugs. She tried to figure out how to make the pillows on the couch look more comfy and less like a showcase. She realized that perhaps, just maybe, she was overreacting a little when Ryan came in and said, "I'm pretty sure most people don't mess their houses up to prepare for a home visit." She laughed loudly at his playful teasing and then flopped on the couch. She laid her head on his lap and he rubbed his fingertips on her scalp.

"Ryan, I can't believe how fast my heart has changed. I am sitting here dreaming about letting our kids play in mud. Thinking about what I would dress a little girl in for church and watching a little boy play baseball."

"Sweetie, I know what you mean. I can't stop thinking about what the future may hold. It's kind of crazy when you think about the fact that not only do we not know if we are having a boy or a girl, but we don't even know how old our child will be when he or she comes to us. We could get a newborn or an eleven-year-old. Do you have an age preference, hon?"

"I just want whatever child God has picked out for us."

"Me too, Jen. Me too."

Ryan then began to pray for their growing family. He prayed for their little one out there right now, probably experiencing less than perfect circumstances now. He asked God to keep the child safe and that they would already feel loved by them, somehow, someway."

When Ryan finished with an affirming amen Jenny asked him to come to the bedroom they hoped to have a child sleeping in soon. They went and looked at the room, which was painted tan. On an impulse, Jenny opened the closet they used for storage in the room, and got a thick permanent marker. She walked over to where she envisioned putting the bed and wrote in big letters and pretty handwriting, "We already love you and we haven't even met you yet." Ryan loved the way his wife was impulsive, and though he was at first startled by her writing on the walls, he loved the message. Then he teased her even more saying, "If our kid writes on the wall, we know where they got it from."

21

Tuesday morning came and the ladies felt like it had been forever since they had been together. They sat down. Lizzy didn't waste much time leading right into the lesson. By now everyone had heard about Deke's truly untimely death.

Lizzy said, "Our original plan was to study the book of Romans 12 pretty much verse by verse in order, but for this week we are going to skip ahead. We are going to hop on over to verse 15. 'Rejoice with those who rejoice and mourn with those who mourn.' Ya know, it occurred to me that we are all in so many different parts of our lives. I never want one of you to be afraid to talk about your circumstances because of what you are facing. Just today we have Monica mourning the loss in her life, yet Jenny is celebrating, rejoicing, if you will, a new addition in their life sometime soon."

Kate chimed in, "Yeah, it's like, we need to be there for our friends, no matter what. It's okay if we laugh and dance and then cry in the same Bible study."

Monica smiled a small, timid smile to her friends and said, "It's okay if we rejoice first. Jenny, I want to hear how the home visit went. Tell us all about it. I need to hear something good today."

Jenny felt odd talking about her good news, but Monica said she needed to hear it, and she was excited to tell everyone how well yesterday had gone. "Well, first off, you all know that while I can cook tofu better than most, that my baking skills are not so hot, right? Well, I decided to try and bake some cookies before the social work lady got there. I figured even I could handle the cookies in a tube from the refrigerator section at the store. Well, she got there about ten minutes early and about fifteen minutes into our meeting, we smelled smoke. I ran to the kitchen as fast as I could to shut the oven off. I made the mistake of opening up the oven door and big billows of smoke came out, setting off the smoke alarm. "

"You've got to be kidding us," Kate was laughing so hard. "What did the lady say?'

Jenny laughed as she remembered her reaction. "Well, at least I know your smoke detectors work now and I can check that off your home study form!"

"I was so relieved that she didn't dock points off for that. I'm glad we all got a good chuckle out of it. And of course she passed when I offered her some of the cookies!"

Jenny said the meeting was very easy and relaxed. She had an instant connection with her caseworker, whose name was Missy. They spent a good part of the meeting filling out paperwork, explaining their desire to adopt, and talking about the clearances and home studies that would need to occur before placement.

"I was surprised at how much was involved, but she gave me a checklist, which will help keep us moving in the right direction. The only thing she gave us that is a little daunting is a background questionnaire. Both Ryan and I have to fill out a ten-page history about ourselves. She assured us that is the hardest part. That's my afternoon goal after Bible study."

"Ten pages?" Lizzy inquired. "What in the world are those questions about?"

"Oh, things like our education, work background, experience with kids, what we do in our spare time, even things like how we get along with our siblings and parents. It's pretty intense."

"So, what was the general feeling you got from meeting the social worker?" Kate asked.

"I felt like she was really happy to be working with us. She seemed to connect with us. She loved the picture I have hanging up with all of you in it. She asked if you were my sisters. She talked about the frustrations of the foster to adopt program. She said they never really have a timeline. The only thing she seemed uneasy about was that we hadn't narrowed down an age group. We promised her that we were open to any age group."

Blair commented, "So, you are not just looking to adopt a baby?"

"Well, we would love a baby. But, we also want to keep in mind that there are several older kids that need good homes too. Missy told us that when kids reach the age of four, their adoptability drops immensely."

"Wow, I guess I never thought of that," Blair replied. "Jenny, I'm so proud of you. It's amazing to see how much your face lights up about this. I'm really, really proud of you." Blair felt like getting to see the change in Jenny was a real chance for them to bond, with the whole group really. She was finally able to encourage someone and remark about how they were growing. This was her chance to see something start, and not just to see its middle or end. It made her feel very close with all of them.

Lizzy took a really big breath and looked at Monica. "Monica, do you want to talk about how you are doing?"

Monica smiled and said, "With a group of friends like you, who pray the way you do, it would be foolish of me not to talk."

Now it was Monica's turn to take a deep breath. "Well, the drive up there was very special. Jer really bonded with Mandy. I had fun just being in the car with him, even though we were going to see Deke. Jer really made me feel safe. Well, as we started to get closer, I got an uneasy feeling. I knew something was wrong. So, when I saw Sandy sitting on the porch, I just got out of the car. And she told me. He had died, while we were driving up there." Monica started to cry, and Blair, who was sitting on the pink couch next to her, handed her a tissue from the end table. Monica took a moment to compose herself and continued on. "The hardest part was trying to explain to Mandy. She thought we were all crying because of how Deke had treated me. Finally, Jer had taken her aside and told her what had happened. I mean, Jer handled everything so well. He was really the only one thinking straight. He was awesome. But, I guess this isn't about Jer, now is it?" She blushed.

Jenny, always trying to lighten the mood said, "It can be if you want."

All five women giggled, thankful for the comic relief that Jenny provided on a regular basis.

"After Jer had explained to Mandy what had happened and then helped console all three of us a little bit, we decided that everyone could use a little something to eat. Sandy was so upset that she hadn't cooked for us. But, of course that didn't matter to us. Actually, it would have been weird to eat there right then. So, we headed to Pizza Hut. Believe it or not, I worked there for a few months when I was pregnant with Mandy. Well, anyways, we went there to grab a pizza. While we were there, Sandy told me something amazing about Deke. It turns out that right after he got sick, he went to a church to pray. Sandy told me she was amazed because she had asked him for years to go to church with no success. Actually, so did I. But, anyways, he walked into a church, listened to a sermon about salvation, and asked Jesus to forgive him of his sins that very day. She said his transformation was dramatic and he immersed himself in going to Bible studies and meeting with the pastor at that church. Sandy also said that she even stopped going to her little old church on Main Street so she could spend more time with Deke. I guess it was a really sweet time for them."

"Woah, no way!" Jenny was amazed. Out of all the women, Jenny probably knew the most about what had happened with Monica and Deke and how amazing it was that he had ever turned to the Lord.

"Way. True Story. So, yeah, I guess this went on for about six weeks before Deke really started getting super sick. So, then Sandy said he started getting depressed about the things he had done in the past. He had nightmares almost every night. And sometimes he would cry out in his sleep for Mandy. Sandy really had to push him to face the facts, but she said, the day he decided to write that letter to send to me, a peace came over him. He was so excited to see Mandy and to apologize to me."

Suddenly, Monica burst into tears. "Mandy never got to say good-bye. He never got to see what a good girl she is. Not that he deserved it. But it's not even a possibility now. There's no hope for Mandy to ever even really remember a good memory of her dad."

Jenny slid Monica's hand into hers. It was shaking from the sudden outburst of emotion. "Honey, Mandy's a good kid. And she's learned forgiveness from her momma. You are the best forgiver I know. She's gonna be okay. And, just think, maybe Mandy will have a good memory of her dad. Maybe she'll have lots of them?"

"What? He's gone, Jenny. *Gone!*" Monica was frustrated with intense emotion.

"Jer, Jer, sweetie," Jenny whispered it.

And poor Monica just started crying all over again.

The rest of the group huddled around her. Each took a turn praying one by one about Mandy, Monica, and the loss they were enduring. Blair said it best, "God, I know this has been a continual loss in Monica's life for a long time. Now it's a loss that has been finalized. Please, help her come to terms with that. And help us help her along the way. Please, Lord. Please."

Lizzy finished up the prayer circle and added a special prayer in there for Monica's future. "God, even though this part of Monica's past is gone, help her future be bright, please. Please let Jer be what she's been waiting for."

Monica cried for a while more after they were done praying. In fact, Lizzy told her to lie down on the couch. Monica, too tired to argue, obeyed. Blair covered her up with the throw blanket from the back of the couch and the other ladies quietly made their way to the kitchen. They made tea and sat around the table talking for a couple of hours. Since Monica was fast asleep, Lizzy made a quiet phone call making sure that Nancy or Carl would be home to get Mandy off the bus. Nancy was home and reassured Lizzy that Gramma and Mandy would enjoy some quality time together while Monica rested. Then, she tiptoed in to the living room and looked at Monica's cell to get Jer's number. She called Jer and let him know that Monica was there and could probably use some extra support when she woke up. "Of course I'll be right there. Thanks for taking care of her, Lizzy," Jer responded.

"We'd do anything for this girl," Lizzy said back.

"Me too. Me too."

Monica was sleeping exceptionally longer than anyone had planned. Jer had arrived around 4:00 p.m. and here it was was 6:45

p.m. and she had not woken up yet. Lizzy was enjoying talking to Jer.

"So, Jer, tell me about you. Have you ever been married before?"

"Actually, no, I graduated high school, went to college, and started med school. I had always planned to focus on my career and not start a family until my career was well established. I thought that my vocation was the best way to serve God. As time went on, the financial side of thing became more and more daunting to me. I could not figure out how to survive without living on the streets. So, I switched my program, took the remainder of my classes at a pharmacy school. I graduated six years sooner than I would have with my medical degree, and poured myself into my job. I love helping the people. I was amazed by how relational you could be with people just from filling their prescription bottles. It's been pretty amazing."

"I remember Monica telling me that you really seem passionate about your job." Lizzy smiled at Jer.

"Oh, I am. But, no job can fill the emptiness of a family. I really have felt led to pursue a family. The dating site seems so hokey at first, but I really like it because I was able to skip over all that who-is-this-person kind of stuff. Ya know what I mean."

Lizzy laughed. "Actually, no. I have no clue, but I'm glad it worked for you! I can't believe that actually worked for someone I know. I've only heard horror stories about all the online dating."

"Well, it has helped me meet Monica, so to say it worked for me would be an understatement." Jer blushed as he said it. "We were really careful. You have to be with that kind of thing. Ya know?"

He was so thankful that Monica had such good friends. They really encouraged her, and really took care of her. Ryan came home shortly after that conversation and Jer enjoyed talking about sports with him while Lizzy put the final touches on dinner.

The beef stroganoff smelled amazing. Lizzy had also made homemade mashed potatoes. She was using her hand masher for the first time in years, as she was being careful not to wake Monica. Buttered peas and sweet tea rounded out the meal.

"I love this woman for all sorts of reasons, but her cooking is right at the top of the list," Ryan joked.

Lizzy loved how amiable and jovial her husband was. And she

loved how someone new to their home could feel so comfortable. Truthfully, she was grateful that Jer was as relaxed of a person as he was too. He just seemed so perfect for Monica, who at times could be so worried about the tiniest little things.

While the guys talked more, Lizzy let her mind wander. She remembered one time when Monica worried about mailing a bill in late. She was convinced that she had forgotten to put a stamp on it, and as a result, was certain that she would be charged extra fees and the company would be furious at her. She seriously fretted about that so much, and she was not satisfied until she saw the check had been cashed. She had wasted so much time that week logging online to her bank account to see if it had made it to the bill center. She had even called and explained the situation to the company, who assured her that they would forgo a late fee if it didn't make it them in time. Lizzy had been there when Monica had called. She could barely talk because she was so concerned about the bill being late. So many things like that, which seemed silly to the rest of them, would trip Monica up. But, all her sweetness made up for that quirky little habit. And, honestly, Lizzy had noticed that Jer seemed to relax Monica.

They were just finishing up dinner when they heard Monica crying in the other room. Jer and Lizzy headed into the living room. She was sitting up, but her head was down in a pillow, just sobbing. They each picked a side of her, and put their arms around her shoulders just to let her know that they were there.

She was disoriented, almost as if she was still half asleep. Monica was saying scattered words about a dream she had and how everything felt so big. When Jer spoke, Monica startled.

"Jer?" she asked. "Jer, you're here? I thought you had died too." And she began crying all over again. "Where's Mandy? *Where's Mandy?*"

"Honey, take a deep breath. Why don't you just take a nice deep breath with me and we will explain everything, ok? It's okay. You just fell asleep here." Lizzy reassured her friend, calmly, carefully, and slowly.

Monica took a nice deep breath and blew out slowly. "That's it. Take another one." Lizzy directed.

Monica obeyed, and quickly she regained her composure.

As she settled down and looked around the room, she just looked at Jer, and then kind of flopped over into his arms. She finally was able to get out what her dream had been about.

"Jer, I dreamt you died too. And I was going to be all alone again."

"Hon, you are okay. I'm okay. God's got us right where he wants us. K?"

"Mmm-hmmm"

"Ok," Jer added. His heart broke for this woman.

"I think the hardest part is knowing that Mandy will never get to speak to him again, never have chance for redemption." Monica said softly.

"I know, but God is good. And we have the promise that Deke did change his life at the end. And you always have that letter to show Mandy. How he had wanted to see her and how he wanted to make things right before he went, right?" Jer tried his best to reassure her.

As Lizzy watched the interaction, she could only feel excitement. She knew she should be mourning right now for Monica, but really all she could do was rejoice. Because even though she had lost one part of her life, she had a brand-new life starting right in front of her, with a guy who just seemed perfect for her. Jer was a gift straight from God. There was no doubt in her mind about it.

She excused herself and let Jer and Monica work through the painful emotions of the last few days. And she went in and found Ryan. "Oh, Ryan, I love watching young love. I love how they are just perfect for each other."

Ryan smiled at her and said, "Yeah, but I love how seasoned love works. I love sharing my life with a beautiful woman who has forgiven me more than any woman should." He walked over to her, wrapped his strong arms around her, and gave her a tender kiss.

She laughed and said, "I love you too. And I love how you said seasoned instead of old."

22

Kate was a mess. She was weaker than normal and had been sleeping more than she ever had before in her life. She could barely get the energy to eat. She wanted to ask her friends to pray for her appointment this afternoon, but she just felt too much fear to bring it up. There was already so much emotion in the room at Bible study today, and she didn't feel like adding to it. Her mother-in-law was watching the kids after school today. Her appointment wasn't until 3:30, so she had enjoyed an extra-long visit at Lizzy's after Bible study, and then she went to a coffee shop to take a time out. She brought her Bible in, and enjoyed time with the Lord and her tea and doughnut, all three sweet in its own way. She had prayed to God about what the doctor was going to say. She knew something was wrong. She hadn't felt like herself. No matter how hard she tried, her mind kept going back to when Jenny was diagnosed with cancer. She knew that was a dramatic leap, but watching one of your friends suffer through that will do that to you. She had actually even shared her concerns with the receptionist at her doctor's, and they asked her to have some blood work done before she came in.

Despite the amount of prayers she had prayed that day, Kate was still scared. She arrived at the doctor's office twenty minutes early. She waited in the waiting room for fifteen minutes. They seemed like hours. She tried to busy herself with *Ladies' Home Journal* and *Wom-*

en's World, but it did no good. Then she watched the looping medical advertisements on the TV. They annoyed her as they listed more and more things that could be wrong with her. "Maybe I have lupus," she thought.

Then, like always, she chastised herself. "Get ahold of yourself. Whatever is wrong is probably something simple. Maybe you just have low iron. Just stop the ridiculous hypochondriac routine."

The nurse came out and smiled sweetly at her when she stood up after hearing her name. The smile gave her a weird feeling. She knew her blood work definitely showed something now. They walked back on the scale. Kate was horrified to see she had gained six pounds since she had been here.

"Well, that's embarrassing," she muttered.

The nurse just patted her shoulder. "Sometimes that happens, Dear."

They went to the room. The nurse took her vital signs. Her blood pressure was slightly elevated.

"Are you nervous?" she inquired.

Kate took a deep breath and nodded her head.

"It's all going to be okay, sweetie. I promise." Kate took that reassurance as more proof that she surely had something wrong with her.

"The doc will be in in just a few minutes." She smiled again and was gone.

The wait from the nurse to the doctor passed by slowly, though Kate knew it had only been about four minutes. She examined the eye chart up on the wall. She tried to form words from the letters present on the sign. She took deep breaths trying to lower her blood pressure. She tried to remember a Psalm she had read in the coffee shop that had made her feel safe. But, all the distractions she tried did not work. By the time the doctor had walked in she had tears in her eyes and had braced herself for the worst.

The doctor walked in with a big, bright smile on her face. She was the nicest doctor Kate had ever met. She really cared about each patient. Her name was Dr. Amy. She remembered not only her name, but she remembered all about Phil and the boys. She often wished that Dr. Amy was a close personal friend and not just her doctor.

"Hi, Kate, it's always so nice to see you. So, it says here in my chart that you've made this appointment because you've been feeling pretty run-down. Pretty weak, is that right?"

Kate said, "Yeah, more tired than I can ever remember being."

"Well, sometimes pregnancy does that to an expectant mom." The doctor said matter-of-factly.

"But, I'm not pregnant, doctor. We've been trying for almost a year, and I'm not pregnant."

The doctor smiled and said, "Kate, I thought that was why you were here! When I ran your labs, I saw that you were pregnant! I didn't know that you didn't know!"

"What? I haven't thrown up or anything like I did with the boys." Kate was completely puzzled.

"Well, like I said, sometimes certain moms just present symptoms of exhaustion. I'm judging by the fact that this is a complete surprise that you do not have any idea how far along you are, is that correct?"

Kate just nodded. She had always been irregular, so she had always judged by symptoms if she was pregnant.

"Well, let's run some more blood work and maybe get you set up with an ultrasound appointment, k?" The doctor left the room quickly and gave the information to the receptionist to make the appointment. When Dr. Amy came back in, she tried to make sure she understood what was happening.

"So, you are telling me I don't have cancer or lupus, right? You are telling me I am having a baby?"

Dr. Amy laughed and said, "Kate, never for a second did either of those diseases cross my mind. Yes! You are indeed carrying a baby!" Kate had already been so full of emotion from worry and self-diagnosis that she had no emotional control left.

She started to cry. "I can't believe it! I've wanted this so badly, so very badly."

"I know! I'm so happy for you. I love seeing my patients have their dreams realized." Dr. Amy just beamed watching Kate take in the good news.

The receptionist knocked on the door and handed Kate an appointment card for Thursday morning. It was a day and a half away.

She was not certain she could wait that long. After a quick exam, she got up and Dr. Amy gave her a hug. "I'm leaving here feeling completely different than I had expected" Kate joked.

The doctor assured her, "Just relax and enjoy this beautiful surprise."

As Kate walked out of the office, she thought of the verse they had studied that morning. Talk about rejoicing and mourning, all at the same time. Kate had just lived both of those out today, in her own little mind.

How would she tell Phil? Would he be as excited now as when they first started trying to conceive? What would the boys think? For the last few months, Kate had given up hope. Infertility haunted her thoughts at all times. She had just set her mind on the fact that she had two boys to love on and that maybe she wasn't meant to have any more. Truth be told, people were not that sensitive to a women who was having difficulty trying to conceive when she already had children. Their words cut like a knife. "Just be thankful for the kids you have."

So many times she had wanted to speak back to them the way they had to her. "I *am* thankful for my kids, thank you very much. I love them so much that I want more." She was thankful for the self-control that God had given her in those moments, but sometimes she would have done anything to enlighten those snarky people, some of them even from church, to the fact that they desired to have a baby to raise in the hope of the Lord from day one. So few understood that, but her Bible study girls understood. And Phil understood. Actually it was his idea.

She remembered the night he suggested it. They were putting away some of the boys' baby toys shortly after they had first turned to the Lord. They had just cancelled their satellite subscription, so they had been talking more, reading more as a family, and Phil even started helping around the house. He had found one of Damian's loveys from when he was a baby. It was soft blue fuzz on one side, with a silk smooth satin backing on the other. He had picked it up remembering how he loved holding his little baby boys.

"Honey, how amazing would it be to have a baby now that we are following the Lord? Do you think things would be different? Can you imagine praying over a little baby as you rocked them to sleep?"

"I could," she responded. "And actually, there are few things in the world I would like more."

That was almost a year ago, and now, she would get to share the good news with Phil.

When she got home, she decided to run up to the attic. Phil and the boys were playing in the back yard, so she had time to do it unnoticed. She went up to the tote where she had stored that little lovey. She carefully, very carefully, climbed back down the attic ladder and went into her bedroom. She grabbed a piece of paper out of her study Bible on the nightstand and wrote Phil a note. "Our dream is coming true. Love, K." It would be so hard to wait for him to find it, but she thought that little lovey would say it best.

She was even more thankful when she thought about how Phil had been going to the Bible study and the boys were responding to his method of handling things so much better. Even though their house was still chaotic, it had peacefulness to it that it had never had before, a house full of love and peace. Who could ask to bring a new baby into anything more?

She realized that since she knew the cause of her weakness, she was much more able to put it aside this evening. She cooked some spaghetti for dinner, and threw some frozen meatballs and garlic bread in the oven. Her boys would all be excited for that dinner.

They came in, all three dirty, smelly and sweaty from their outside adventures. She suggested to all three of them to take showers before dinner. Without much thought about it, they headed upstairs. Suddenly, she heard Phil scream. "What? Honey! Come here! Come here!"

Kate took off upstairs wondering what could be upsetting him so much. As she entered the room, she realized he was not upset at all, but rather he had found the lovey on his pillow and was quite literally jumping up and down.

"Kate, is this why you haven't felt good? Did you tell me that just to throw me off! That isn't nice."

"No, honey. I really, really thought something was wrong. The doctor ran all that blood work and told me this morning! I was so surprised. I know this sound ridiculous, but I had prepared myself to be dying."

"Kate, you have to learn to just relax, honey. But, I'm so glad that we are having a baby!" She had not seen Phil this excited in a long time.

"Phil, if you can take an hour off of work, we get to go to the ultrasound lab on Thursday morning. Do you want to come?"

"Of course I do! We asked God for this baby, and sure enough, he answered our prayers. Do you know when you are due yet?" Phil asked.

"Nope, I haven't a clue. The doctor said we will know after measuring the baby."

Phil picked up the lovey again, and held it against his chest. He bowed his head in prayer.

"God, thank you for giving us a brand-new life. Thank you for changing us, and for giving us this new baby. I can't believe this is really happening. God, we are so excited. Thank you."

Today, it was a day of rejoicing.

23

Blair was so thankful for the little Bible study. It had become one of the highlights of her week, along with learning how to spend time with the Lord and her family. Her kids had noticed the way Blair had been learning from Romans 12, and they began talking about all kinds of new things. Their family had started to look much different. Instead of watching TV before bed, they were playing games and reading the Bible. Blair realized that to raise children in a way that pleased God, there needed to be so much more interaction than just staring at a screen together. Samuel felt the same, and as they sprung into the time of year where holidays approached, their family had a bigger sense of togetherness than ever. Thankfulness was no longer just celebrated at Thanksgiving, but they were celebrating it every single day while praying, and while being together.

She asked her family to pray for Monica. They all had heard about what happened to Monica's ex-husband at church on Sunday. They prayed earnestly for their hurting friend. As everyone was finishing up before bedtime routines, the phone rang.

"Sam, hon, can you take care of the rest of the schedule tonight? It's Carlee!"

"Go, talk. Enjoy!" Sam assured her he had it all under control.

"Carlee! I'm so excited to hear from you! It's been so long!"

Carlee didn't seem as excited as Blair when she replied, "You know, the phone works both ways."

The phone line was silent for a second. Blair wasn't expecting that kind of tone from her friend.

They had been neighbors in North Carolina. They had lived in an old little neighborhood where all the houses were right next door to each other. They could wave at each other from their kitchen windows and often they would meet on Blair's back deck after their kids had gone to bed for the night. They had done everything together. They had celebrated birthdays, holidays, pregnancies, and had even worked through Carlee's miscarriage together. The move had been hard on her, Blair knew that. But, Carlee was a secure person, with a lot of friends, and Blair figured that she would bounce back quickly. Apparently, things had not been going as well for Carlee as Blair had imagined.

"Carlee, are you okay?" Blair asked the question full of concern.

"I'm fine," she snapped. Then she added, "But, I see your Facebook posts and updates and pictures. You have a brand-new life in Tennessee. You never call me anymore. You hardly even e-mail me. You have all these new friends from this Bible study group all of a sudden. Do you think you are holier than me now? Do you think you are better than me? Is that why you never even contact me anymore?" Carlee was mad, and she was on a roll.

"Carlee, I guess I'm just getting settled in here. I'm trying to figure out who I am. How I want to serve God where I am right now."

"See, that's what I'm talking about. You would have never talked like that before. You are going all strange. Who are you? You are not the same anymore, Blair. You left and now you have gone and changed who you are."

"Car, I haven't changed who I am. Not really. I'm the same person. I'm just learning so much about God. I can't follow God, realizing how much he loves me and not be changed." She sighed. She had not realized how much she had changed. But, things were different. "I guess maybe I am not the same. But, I think I'm a better version of me. "

"See, I knew you thought you were better than me." Carlee was not making any sense.

"Carlee, I never said that. I said I'm a better *me*. Not that I'm better than you. Let's face it, we are all sinners anyways."

"So, now you are calling me a sinner? Seriously, who are you? You are a completely different person."

And with that, she heard a click. And the conversation was over.

She sat down, and tears started falling. She never thought that following Jesus could cause something like this to happen.

After Samuel finished putting the kids into bed, he came into their room and saw her crying on the bed.

"Honey, what's the matter? What are you crying about? Did Carlee have bad news?"

Blair shook her head no. "I just can't believe her. She accused me of referring to myself as better than her. She made me feel like the worst friend ever. She took everything I said out of context and then she hung up on me. Seriously, Samuel, she hung up on me like kids do in high school."

Samuel was shocked. That did not sound like the Carlee he knew either.

"Did she say anything else?"

"No, she just started off complaining about how I hadn't called her. And then she freaked out. And then, like I said, she hung up. I tried to explain to her, but she simply hung up."

"Wow. Hey, Blair, I don't want to sound weird or anything, but do you know what this kind of reminds me of?"

"What, hon?"

"It kind of reminds me of one of the verses in the Bible chapter you've been reading."

He walked over and grabbed a Bible from the bookshelf in their room. It was one that Samuel's grandmother had given him when he was just a little boy. Even though Samuel had gone to church his whole life, and had done many spiritual things, the reading the Bible at home thing was still new to him too.

He opened up to Romans 12 and read the verse, "Bless those who persecute you; bless and do not curse."

"Okay, so I don't want to sound like a pastor or anything, but, sweetie, the easy thing would be to turn against her. How about if we pray for her? And maybe you can pray that God will show you a specific way to bless her?" Samuel was treading lightly. He was not used to being a spiritual leader, at least in this sense, in their home. And he knew how sensitive his sweet wife could be at times.

"I think that is something we could try." Blair was skeptical, but she wanted to do something that would please God.

"Dear Lord, I pray for Carlee right now. God, I know that she was super upset tonight. God, I know I have changed a lot over the last couple of months. I can praise you for that. I hope that Carlee can someday too." Suddenly, Blair had a big feeing of conviction come over her. "God, I just realized that even though I knew you when we lived in North Carolina, I didn't live for you. I didn't even talk to you, or about you or anything. I'm sorry for that."

Blair stopped praying for a minute and let her mind wander back to North Carolina. What had they talked about all those nights on the porch? Well, there was neighborhood gossip to catch up on, of course. They complained about in-laws. They laughed about cute things their kids did. They compared notes about what they were working on for the PTO. They discussed birthday presents, trips to the zoo, and sometimes even complained about their husbands. But, never, ever, not once did Carlee and Blair talk about God. It was an unspoken. Blair went to church. Carlee didn't. And they simply never talked about it.

"God, how could I have been best friends with someone for over seven years and never shared how much you love her too? Oh, Lord, I'm so sorry."

As Blair cried her lamentations over so many missed opportunities, Samuel took over praying.

In his deep, soothing voice he prayed, "God, thank you for bringing us here. Thank you for changing us. Thank you for breaking us free from the way we used to be. We pray for Carlee. That she will feel your love. God, we pray the new neighbors that will buy our house will be believers and share your love with her. Or that someone else will come into her life. And also that you can still use Blair. Please, help Blair reach out to Carlee and help their relationship to be mended. Oh, yeah, and Lord, please help that house sell. Amen"

As they finished praying, Blair looked up at the clock. She still had time to make a quick phone call. As she picked up the phone, Samuel asked, "Are you going to call her back."

SARAH ROSE

Blair shook her head and walked over to the computer and googled a phone number.

Her fingers were a little twitchy as she dialed the phone number. "Hello, Corner Café. This is Marcy speaking."

"Hi, Marcy. This is Blair Stevens. Do you remember me?"

"*Blair*! How could I ever forget you!? You just moved away a few months ago, not forty years ago. How are you honey?"

"Oh, Marcy, I miss you and your sweet coffee shop. I miss those cinnamon rolls. That's for sure!"

"Well, honey, I sure do miss your face around these parts. You know, Carlee still comes in just about two or three times a week, and orders the same thing as you both always have."

Blair smiled. Yes, this is what she wanted. "So, Marcy, I was wondering if you would help me out with a little surprise for Carlee. Can I send you a check to cover about a month of coffee and cinnamon rolls for her? And some messages for you to deliver to her. Being apart is hard on us. I miss her, and I just want to let her know I still love her."

"Oh, bless your heart, Blair. You always were the sweetest girl." Marcy's thick southern drawl really stood out while on the phone. "You just send whatever you want here and I'll be happy to help anyway I can."

"Marcy, thank you for being so sweet."

"Anything for a neighbor, dear. Once a neighbor, always a neighbor." Marcy truly embodied southern hospitality.

"Thanks, Marcy. Thank you a million times over."

Blair sat down right away and began making little notes. "I miss having chai lattes with you." "Do you remember that time the duck followed us into the café?" "Once a neighbor, always a neighbor." "No matter how you may feel right now, I promise I'm not judging you. I am just letting God change me." She wrote about twenty different messages and enclosed a letter to Marcy, thanking her again for her help. She included a check for twelve cinnamon rolls and chai lattes, which had been their signature order when they went in. And, just because Marcy was blessing her so much, she included a pretty sizable tip too. She had it stamped and read toy go for the morning.

126

24

Jenny had finally finished her questionnaire from the adoption agency. It was tiring and it had taken almost six hours over the course of two different days. But, she kept telling herself that ever expectant parent had to be uncomfortable along the way. She would never spend that last few weeks pregnant, unable to tie her shoes or see her feet, but she did need to spend hours explaining her history, her background and her desire to be a parent. And she was actually okay with that. She felt like she was earning her way into motherhood.

Ryan, however, did not. Ryan had become increasingly irritable as he filled out the questionnaire. Compared to Jenny's sweet and simple past, Ryan's looked like a sordid mess. His father had abandoned their family, his mother, now recovered and walking with the Lord, had once been a drug addict and an alcoholic. Ryan had to admit on that questionnaire that in his youth, he had been fired from a job for stealing money. He had paid back the money, and then some, plus did community service for a year to make up for that. "I'm so sick of this stupid questionnaire. I'm not this person anymore. I hate this."

Jenny tried to explain her viewpoints on the questionnaire and that made Ryan even angrier. "No! This is ridiculous. We are just trying to help a kid. Someone can go make a kid no matter who they are and what their background is, and here we are trying to make a difference in the world and they treat us like we are criminals. I'm not sure I can do this."

Missy had warned them both that the questionnaire was one of the hardest parts about the adoption process. "Just stick with it and get it done as fast as you can. It is a big part of our screening process." Jenny reminded him of that.

He said with a gruff attitude, "Fine. I'll go finish the thing."

Jenny had hardly ever seen Ryan like that. They had talked about his past, but only in small doses. She prayed for him as he finished the last three pages of the survey. She knew this was difficult. Suddenly she had an idea. While he was working on his form in the other room, Jenny did something she used to do for him all the time when they were dating.

She walked over to the closet where she stored the craft supplies. She grabbed a couple of different colored markers, a blank piece of printer paper and some stickers.

She started by doodling "Jenny loves Ryan" all over the paper with hearts placed around. Then, right in the middle, she wrote one of the verses that she had studied with her Bible study girls. "Never be lacking in zeal, but keep your spiritual fervor, serving the Lord." She smiles as she looked at that verse, but she couldn't stop there. She kept writing the next verse too. "Be joyful in hope, patient in affliction, and faithful in prayer." Those were verses 11 and 12, but she could have kept going through most of the chapter. She then wrote a little note down at the bottom. "My sweet Ryan, God put this desire in your heart. Keep going. You can do this. I'm so proud you are my man, and that you will be the father of our child." She decorated it a little more. Even though the note looked juvenile, she thought it conveyed what she was going for very well. God had called them to walk this road and He would help them get through it.

With a bounce in her step, she walked into the study where he was working. "Ryan, hunny. I have a present for you." She teased him in a sweet, singsong kind of voice. Despite his bad mood, he couldn't help but smile a little at her. She handed it to him and said, "You read this and I'm going to go pray for you while I exercise. Okay?"

He nodded and she exited quickly, went downstairs, and hopped on her elliptical. She loved exercising and praying at the same time. She felt like those moments encapsulated who she was most, a child of God who wanted to be as healthy as she could while she was here on earth. And when she was exercising she could just talk to God the way she really was. At other times when she prayed, she felt like she got caught up in her words or how to say something. When she was exercising, the words came easy and she didn't have to think too much in order to tell God how she was feeling. So, while she was swishing back and forth on her machine, her mind went back and forth from worshipping God, to praising Him for her wonderful husband and then to their unknown child. She prayed for her friends easily, and lifted up Monica particularly. She worked through the verses they had been studying in her mind. Out loud said, "God, I never realized I could use your word this much in my life. Every day I can find new ways to apply this chapter to what I'm going through. Thanks for making such a cool chapter like Romans 12. I'm really thankful that you care enough about me and my friends to lead us to study this chapter." She had to slow down just a little bit to start singing. "Your love is amazing, steady, and unchanging. Your love is a mountain firm beneath my feet. Hallelujah, hallelujah, hallelujah. Your love makes me sing." Ryan came down the stairs quietly and startled her.

"Well aren't you something, Miss Jenny?" he said teasing her. "Not only can you change my mood around with just a little note, but I come down here and see you rocking out worshipping the Lord on your elliptical and now I actually feel like singing with you."

He went to give her a kiss and she pushed him away saying, "Ryan, I'm sweaty and gross."

He kissed her anyway, "I don't care how sweaty you are. I love you. Thanks for reminding me about staying strong. Oh, and by the way, I finished. Thanks, honey."

She smiled at him and started the skiing movements on the elliptical again. Then, just for fun, they both started singing the song as loud as they could.

25

Kate and Phil dropped the boys off at school on Thursday morning. Her appointment was not until ten o'clock so they had a few minutes to go out for breakfast. Phil suggested a tiny little diner that served made from scratch breakfasts and Kate was glad to go with him. While she was not hungry, she was happy to have someone else cook a meal for Phil they way he enjoyed. She hadn't felt like cooking much. She still felt exhausted, as if she could sleep an extra three hours a day.

When they got to the diner, Phil took full advantage of the home cooked menu. He ordered an omelet, with a side of bacon, and a short stack of pancakes. The waitress turned to Kate, ready and waiting for her order. "I'll take a bagel and cream cheese with a cup of tea please." The waitress giggled under her breath at the vast difference of their orders. And Phil smiled like a little kid when she brought the plates filled with food out.

They enjoyed their time together and chatted while they ate. Kate still had to pinch herself to make sure this was the same man she had been married to a couple of months ago. The change was so dramatic in their lives and she was not used to the way they no longer screamed at each other on a daily basis. Yes, they still fought, and they both had moments were they were hot headed, but it was better. He smiled at her more, walked by and rubbed her shoulders often, and they prayed together, and with the kids a couple of times a day. It was a different life.

They had overcome so much. And sometimes it felt like this baby was a reward for that. She knew it seemed cliché, but life seemed so different, almost like the sky was a brighter shade of blue for them. It was hard to talk about, especially to people who knew them from before and about the kind of marriage they had settled for. It was hard not to feel guilty about all the years of happiness stolen away from their marriage because of selfishness. They had both, for years, demanded what seemed fair from their points of view. It had never occurred to put one another's needs ahead of their own and now that they were doing that, it was crazy how happy they were. Oh well, it was not fair to focus on the past now, not when they had so much right in front of them.

As they finished up Phil, joked about being rolled out of the diner. But, they stood up, walked out hand in hand, and decided to walk the seven blocks to the doctor's office. They were both near giddiness as they strolled along.

When they arrived, the technician was very welcoming and put Kate at ease right away. She put the cold jelly on Kate's belly. Upon studying her stomach, she decided that she did indeed look pregnant. How had she missed it before?

The technician showed them a beautiful strong heartbeat, and then she began taking measurements.

She asked them typical questions, "Do you know the date of your last period."

"It was about five months ago, but I'm always very irregular," Kate answered.

"Do you have any guesses about how far along you are?"

Kate shook her head no. "I have no clue. I'm guessing maybe six or seven weeks along."

The technician smiled at her and said, "Well, you certainly are not a very good guesser!" The baby is measuring at fifteen, maybe even sixteen weeks along. That puts your due date at the beginning of April. I bet you weren't expecting a baby that soon."

"Oh my goodness! I'm almost halfway through, and I didn't even know it!" Kate cried out.

Phil asked, "Can you tell if the baby is a boy or girl yet?"

"No, not quite yet, at least not reliably. In about three to four weeks we should have a pretty good picture and be able to tell."

Phil leaned over and kissed Kate. Every day the news in their life was getting better.

The technician said that she would give the report to the doctor, but she thought everything looked good. She handed Kate a towel and Kate began the tough job of getting all the sticky goop off her belly. Once she was cleaned up and put back together, she asked Phil if it was okay to pray. They bowed their head and thanked God for the news that their baby was healthy and would be here sooner than they ever thought. "Thank you, Lord, for surprises and changes and blessings. You are so good to us." Just as Phil had finished that sentence the technician walked back into the room.

Her face was bright with embarrassment. "I'm so sorry. I thought you had left. I didn't mean to interrupt."

"It's okay, we were just thanking God for this amazing little miracle," Kate responded softly.

The lady turned from red to pink and said, "Well, that's the first time I've ever seen someone praying in here like that. Good for you. I guess this baby is very lucky to be coming into a family like yours, a family who loves the baby even before it gets born." She was obviously very nervous, stumbling over words.

Kate, feeling almost pulled in the technician's direction went over and hugged her. She said, "Thank you for doing what you do. You gave us a chance to see our little one. You make a difference in this world."

Since Kate was already near the door, Phil stood up to leave.

The technician wiped the tears from her eyes. "No one has ever done that before, either."

Phil grabbed Kate's hand on the way out. "Yes, ma'am, God has given us this baby. And we are going to raise him or her in a completely different way, right from the start. And what a start today was. I'm proud of you, honey, and I'm so glad this is who we are now."

They walked, almost skipping the blocks to where they had parked the car. Now was the fun part. It was time to tell others!

26

Another week had gone by. As Lizzy's couch and chairs filled up the Tuesday before Thanksgiving, the group was busy chatting about holiday plans and their favorite tried and true recipes. Lizzy heart hurt a little as she realized this was the first Thanksgiving she would be without her boys. Both of them had to stay back at college this year. She was proud of her sons and what they had accomplished, and how they both were self-sufficient. Both worked jobs that needed them to stay behind. It would be a lonely, quiet Thanksgiving. Actually, with an empty house, and no nearby relatives, she and Brad had decided to go work at the soup kitchen in the morning, and they would just come home and eat a rotisserie chicken purchased from Wal-Mart. She was happy to help out with the needs of the community, but she just felt very isolated this season, especially when she listened to the exciting plans everyone had with their children at home, or in Jenny's case, with her siblings all coming in to town, with her nieces and nephews.

At one point, Lizzy actually had tears flood her eyes. She was thankful for the excuse to go make coffee so she could wipe her eyes in private. She heard someone following her and she tried not to make eye contact with whoever it was. But, Monica, being very sensitive had picked up on the fact that Lizzy was not quite herself today long before the tears had ever snuck up on her.

"Lizzy, I was wondering if you would like to join our family for dinner, you and Brad both. Jer enjoyed his visit with you the other night, and it's the least I could offer after the way you cared for me last week."

"Oh, Monica, you don't have to do that," Lizzy said, trying to refuse.

"Lizzy, you are family to me. Please, don't make me beg. I want you there, and, think how happy Mandy would be if you were there. She misses you so much during the school year. Please, please will you come?"

Lizzy turned around and fell into a sobbing hug. "Oh, Monica, I don't deserve a friend like you. Here you are, still grieving, and I'm imposing on you."

Monica simply responded, "Family is never an imposition, especially family like you."

The meal was set for 4:00 p.m. on Thursday and suddenly Lizzy felt a lot more thankful and much less lonely. She was grateful that God knew what her heart needed. As the coffee finished its aromatic brew, she transferred it to a pretty, white carafe. She refilled creamer and sugar bowls, placed them on the tray and took it out to the living room. "Okay, ladies. We are going to start by thanking God this morning," Lizzy said as she entered the living room from the kitchen. "Three random things, lighthearted or deep, whatever you want. Blair, why don't you start us off?"

"Okay. Three things, new friend, old friends, and my family."

Lizzy smiled at her. "Great! How about you, Monica?"

Monica smiled. "Jer."

Everyone gave a collective "Ahhh! How sweet."

Monica blushed. She continued. "Mandy and my job. I love being able to encourage the students who seem to need it most. I love the substitute role. Just filling in when I'm needed."

Kate smiled at Monica. "You truly are a perfect fit for that job. You are the only substitute I know who would praise God for that position."

Monica responded, "Hey, I've dodged my share of spit wads, but for the most part, you treat the kids with respect, they treat you with respect."

Lizzy was up next. "I am thankful for my husband and sons. I know that is technically three already, but I just have to say how thankful I am for this group. You ladies keep me growing. And, you all make me feel younger than I am!"

"Sometimes I forget that you are even older than us," Jenny remarked.

Lizzy smiled at her comment, and then encouraged Jenny to share her list. "Let's see. I cannot tell you how thankful I am to be almost a year out from all the cancer stuff. I feel free, alive, and grateful for my life every day! And I'm so glad that God has changed my heart and that we are adopting. All the paperwork and clearances are submitted. Now we are just waiting for the licensing to come through so that we can officially be put on the list! And, I guess my last one is kind of silly. But, I'm really, really thankful for fuzzy socks, especially this time of year."

Lizzy giggled and said, "It's the little things, isn't it?"

They all nodded. It was Kate's turn. She thought her turn would never arrive. "Well, I'm so glad Blair has joined our group and I'm not the newbie anymore!" They smiled back and forth at one another. "I'm also thankful for the way Phil and I have been getting along and how the boys' behavior has improved."

"There have been so many great changes in your family this year, haven't there?" Lizzy remarked.

Kate nodded, and took a deep breath. "Oh, yeah, and there's one more thing too. I'm thankful that come April we will be raising another little one!"

"Say *what*?" Jenny screamed.

It took everyone else a couple seconds to catch what she said. They really livened up. Monica even began jumping up and down! Jenny was tearing up for her friend.

"We can raise babies together, maybe?" she said.

Blair hugged her saying, "The third one adds such a fun dynamic to the home! Oh, your boys are going to love being big brothers."

"When did you find out?"

"When are you due again?"

"How far along does that make you?"

"Do you know if it is a boy or girl?"

The questions and excitement filled the room and it was hard to simmer the group down. Actually, Lizzy decided she had no intentions of simmering the group down. This is what Thanksgiving was all about. Letting praises go up to God without holding back, just celebrating life, blessings, and miracles. Just in their little group of five, there was a myriad of things to be thankful for!

While everyone was in the midst of celebrating, Lizzy opened her Bible to the Psalms and read Psalm 118. "Give thanks to the Lord. His love endures forever!"

The conversation continued gleefully, and Lizzy sat there quietly. She prayed for each lady in the group. It was probably another twenty minutes before things died down.

Jenny, in her own, spunky way turned to Lizzy and said, "Okay, Liz. Whatcha got for us today? Anything good?"

"Well, here's the cool thing. I barely have to teach on this verse today, because I think we do such a great job of this in our little group. So, here's the verse:

"When God's people are in need, be ready to help them. Always be eager to practice hospitality." I think that Monica did a perfect job setting an example of this today. In order to know if people are in need, sometimes it takes some extra insight. Monica is a great example of this. She knew I was having a tough time today, without me even telling her. And because she is so sweet, she invited me to share Thanksgiving with her family. Well, me and Brad. I cannot wait to tell Brad. He's going to be so excited! You are keeping us from being home alone eating chicken like it's a regular night."

And all of us at different times have been able to do things like this for each other.

Kate spoke up, "Just like you gifted us with a weekend away a few weeks ago. It was like a dream come true, and now it's even more important that we solidify our marriage as much as we can before we embark on round number three!"

Lizzy was a little embarrassed being used as an example. She turned red, and said, "Well, I guess that is an example too."

"Lizzy, don't be embarrassed. You do it for all of us. You are wonderful. Whether its letting me sleep on your couch, or calling us so we can pray for one of our friends, or just opening your home to us each week, you live this verse out so wonderfully." Monica wanted Lizzy to realize the impact of all her efforts.

Blair chimed in. "Lizzy, you were my first friend here. I can't imagine how different my life would be if you hadn't seen my need and invited me here."

Jenny said, "Oh, Lizzy! We would fall apart without you."

Lizzy had tears in her eyes. She had never really thought that she could make any difference doing what she did. But, apparently, it did matter. She thought about the day on the couch, when she had been crying out to God, asking for the encouragement to keep going, begging Him for the spiritual fervor she needed. She smiled as she realized that these girls were living, breathing tools being used by God to encourage her right at that moment. It was difficult to express to them how she was feeling because of the tears, but she did muster a "Y'all encourage me so much."

27

Thursday morning came, and the same zeal that Lizzy was feeling stir up in her a couple days ago was alive and well in her soul. She rolled out of bed, washed her face, and brushed her teeth. It was early, much earlier than her alarm was scheduled to go off. She had time, so she crawled back into bed and snuggled up with Brad. A series of Thanksgiving prayers echoed in her mind. "Thank you God for this man, for our marriage, for how you have worked in us and through us even though we don't deserve it. Thank you for using me, despite all my shortcomings. Please, Lord, help me and Brad make a difference today. Both at the soup kitchen downtown and also maybe even at Monica's house. Let us live our lives in continual praise of you. Amen."

She cuddled up even tighter to Brad and said, "Happy Thankgiving, Honey! Almost time to get up and make some turkey."

Brad, who rarely slept in past 5:00 a.m. seemed to enjoy the extra hour and a half of sleep. He struggled to get out of bed, but eventually he made it to the shower and in record time they were both ready and off to the soup kitchen. For some reason, Lizzy had expected there to be twenty or thirty people working at the soup kitchen. In reality, there were only six other people besides them. She was worried about how it would all come together in time. Thankfully, three of the group seemed to be veterans at the soup kitchen and they were very organized and good at giving instructions. Lizzy's sole job for the morning was making green bean casserole. She felt like God was being sweet to her, since that was both of her boy's favorite dishes. She loved making it, even if she couldn't serve it to her boys, she would care for another mother's son today. She mixed the cream of mushroom soup in big batches with milk. She added garlic powder and pepper. She made sure to add extra of the French fried onions on the top of each batch, because of course, they were everyone's favorite part. She prayed for each hungry mouth they would feed today. And she hoped that they could fill hungry souls too.

The meals were to be served at 12:30, and the few workers they had in the beginning increased in number. With their crew doubled, they were able to get the meal all finished. They were serving about four hundred people that day. The people needing meals began lining up about 10:30. The dining area was not very big, and only sat about sixty at a time. It was hard to see people, some without coats or gloves or hats, standing outside. It was a very cold Thanksgiving day with temperatures hovering around the freezing mark, and the wind was whipping around furiously. It was difficult to see people looking so bleak on such a happy day as they were standing in line waiting to be served.

Lizzy wondered how they had gotten to the situations they were in. She asked Karlene, the one who seemed to be in charge the most of the preparations, what she knew of people's stories.

Karlene, for the first time that day, stopped preparations. "So many of these people are struggling from alcoholism or years of drug abuse. I know that makes it sound like they are at fault, but so many of these people were raised by families that showed them this was the normal way to live life. They have never experienced the good life, how good things can be. But, there's a fair amount that we will serve today that are families that used to live in decent homes. They may have even fallen into the middle class, but sometimes life throws curve balls you may never expect. One woman, her name is Edie, her husband died unexpectedly from a car accident. Then, about three months later, their mobile home burned down. It was uninsured. With no family in the area, Edie and her three kids have been living from house to house with whoever will take them in for a while, and when they don't have a home, they just live in their car, which is as old as I am, I think."

"Wow. Each person probably has a story uniquely theirs, don't they?" Lizzy inquired.

"They do. They do. And we need to remember that they are people, just like us. We are all a couple of unfortunate events away from being in their shoes. It is heart breaking and humbling."

Lizzy nodded her head and made a very conscience effort to pay attention to people. She wanted to learn about some of them and their stories. At 12:30 when the shelter had all the meals prepared, the doors could open. As the first sixty walked in, Lizzy was not sure what to do with herself. Karlene had put her on crowd control. But since there was someone at the door counting the number of people walking in, she didn't have a lot to do. So, she walked over to a mom who had a crying infant. The mom looked tired. And not just new mom tired. She looked tired, in a hopeless, desperate way. "Hi there, I'm Lizzy. Can I help you with your baby while you get your plate?"

The mom looked at her with sad eyes and handed the baby over to her. "Finally, I've been holding the kid for hours. She won't stop fussing."

"How old is she?" Lizzy asked.

"She's about seven months. Her name is Angel," the mom replied.

Despite the baby's awful stench, which smelled like the body odor of her mother, mixed with cigarettes and spit up, the baby was beautiful. She was dirty but beautiful. She had white curly hair and blue eyes. Her eyes were sad like her momma's. The baby was shivering. The poor thing just had old, worn footie jammies on. "Oh, aren't you a pretty baby?" she cooed.

The mom of the baby just looked away. She didn't say anything. She did not seem to desire to interact with Lizzy anymore. "Well, dear, why don't you fill your plate up, and if you are okay with it, I will walk around with Miss Angel to see if anyone else needs anything."

Lizzy held the baby tightly. She walked over to the back of the room where there was a box of things for children if they came in. There was a blanket there, and a baby hat. She slid the hat on the baby, and wrapped her up in the warm, clean blanket. As Lizzy walked around with the bundle, warming her up, she swayed back and forth, putting baby Angel to sleep. One time, she looked over to Angel's mom. She was eating very fast, shoveling the food in heaps. The woman looked up at Lizzy and then turned her eyes away quickly. Lizzy was concerned about the mom. She seemed jittery, almost like she was waiting for someone to come after her at any minute. Lizzy saw the mom go up to the dessert table for some pie and she met her up there.

"Would you like me to change the baby's diaper for you? I would like to help you any way I can while you are here," Lizzy said sincerely.

The mom smiled almost a half-smile and said that would be nice. "Oh, I don't have any diapers though," the mom said quickly.

Lizzy replied, "You know what? I think they had some in the restroom. I'll go change her while you eat your pie, okay?"

Lizzy walked over to Karlene to double check to make sure the diapers were available to use, and she confirmed that they were. Karlene said, "Lizzy, you are here for a reason. So few volunteers are willing to step on this side of the serving table to do what you are doing today. Holding that baby, giving the mom a break, letting her know she is cared about. This is what really matters today. Thank you."

Lizzy walked Baby Angel back to the restroom. She was thankful that the restroom was small and held heat very well. She undressed the baby and wiped her down the best she could with wipes and the paper towel supply in the restroom. The baby had crusted spit up dried in the creases of her neck, and the more Lizzy cleaned it, the smellier the baby came, not to mention the grumpier. Her neck looked infected once Lizzy had removed the dry, crusted spit up. Red, raw creases were in her neck where the drool had sat for days. When she removed her diaper, she saw the worst diaper rash she had ever seen. That also was inflamed and reeked of infection. The screams from the baby were heart wrenching. Thankfully, there was a tube of Desitin and a box of gloves on the changing table. She was as careful as she could be while cleaning the baby. She put a fresh diaper underneath the baby and sprinkled baby powder on her bottom. She carefully sealed up the fresh diaper and she threw away the other mess, trying not to think about how long the baby had been sitting in her filth. Once the baby's diaper was fastened, the baby began to calm down. Lizzy thought the powder and ointment must feel good to the little peanut. Carefully, she balanced the baby on her hip, alternating as she washed her hands at the sink, one hand at a time. She forgot what a challenge caring for a baby could be, even in the best of circumstances. And here she was struggling even to wash her hands. She couldn't imagine how the baby's mother was managing.

Lizzy walked out of the door, prepared to give the mother the accolades she deserved. However, when she walked out into the dining room, the spot where the mother was sitting was empty. "That's odd," Lizzy thought to herself. I wonder if she went to visit someone. She scanned the room and did not see the lady anywhere.

She walked over to where the woman had been sitting and the only thing that remained was a crumbled napkin. In ink pen, there was a note that said, "I'm done. I've tried my best, but I'm failing her. Please, find her a home. I love her, but this is not the life for her."

"This is not happening. This cannot be happening," Lizzy thought.

She looked for Karlene and found her welcoming more people that came in the door. A few seats had opened up, even though people were reluctant to leave. It was hard to usher those finished with their meals back into the cold, but unfortunately, this small space was all the soup kitchen had to offer. She made her way through the sea of people to Karlene.

"Karlene, she just left. The momma just left her baby. Come read the note. Come, please, read the note."

Karlene went white as a ghost. "Oh, no. That didn't just happen. She did not just leave her baby here!"

Lizzy grabbed Karlene's hand, while cradling the baby with her other hand. "Come and see. She left a note."

Karlene started to shake. The emotions raging through her were indescribable. She had never seen that mom here with her baby before. But, that happened on holidays. You had new people. But, never, ever in all of Karlene's time at the shelter had anything like this happened.

"What do we do?" Lizzy asked?

Karlene looked at her and said, "Well, you keep swaying that baby. She'll be asleep and that will buy us some time. I'll try to get ahold of the police."

"Ok," Lizzy responded. Suddenly, holding this baby was a bigger responsibility than she had ever imagined. Lizzy began to second-guess herself. Had she handled the situation correctly, offering to help the mom? Had she made the mom feel inadequate? Lizzy didn't think so, but she couldn't think straight to remember all the interactions that had taken place with the mom. Even remembering what the mother looked like became increasingly difficult. Suddenly, the only thing she could remember were the dark circles around the woman's eyes. And her hair was dark brown and matted. She remembered that, but nothing else. Lizzy realized that not once had she ever asked the woman's name. She was nameless and faceless in her mind.

Lizzy hurled multiple insults at herself. She started feeling like this little life, now warm and fast asleep in her arms, had been abandoned because of her. "So much for helping the people at the shelter today," she thought. Instead, she had an abandoned baby in her arms. She looked down at the tiny face. Her little lips curved, almost like sideways brackets. They were a very distinctive shape. She had a round nose that was wide for a little baby. But, it was so cute. Her little ears were covered with soft, wispy fuzz. And her golden curly hair still looked beautiful, despite the dirt in the hair and the large amounts of cradle cap on her scalp. She cooed in her sleep and Lizzy couldn't help but wonder what the tiny baby was dreaming about. Without warning, tears started falling from Lizzy's eyes and the first few landed on the baby's cheek, which stirred her slightly from her sleep, but not enough for her to open her eyes. "Oh, Angel, I'm so sorry your momma left you. And I'm so sorry if it's my fault."

Karlene came out of the tiny office and said the police would be there shortly, but a social worker from Children and Youth Services would also come. Whoever got there first, Lizzy would have to be prepared to answer many questions. Karlene then put her hand around Lizzy's shoulder. "Lizzy, this is not your fault. You did everything you were supposed to. You even checked in with me. We just have to trust that somehow God can bring good out of this situation." Lizzy tried to smile at the woman who was working so hard to bring her consolation, but it was not happening. "Let's go see if we can find your husband, ok?"

They found Brad in back washing dishes. "He's a good man," Karlene joked. Lizzy nodded and even smiled a little.

Brad grinned and said, "Well, looky, looky. Who's this little angel?"

Lizzy said, "Actually, her name is Angel."

When Lizzy spoke, Brad looked at her and realized that she had been crying.

"Honey, what's going on?" he asked.

Lizzy started crying again, so Karlene told him the story. She added quietly, "Lizzy is worried it is her fault, although, she did exactly what she should have. She was helping a mom get a nice meal so she could be refreshed and take care of her daughter. Neither Lizzy or I could have imagined the mom would leave."

"Woah." Brad did not have anything else to add, so Karlene continued.

"I've been doing this long enough to know that you cannot allow yourself to feel responsible for someone else's actions. I assure you, Lizzy, that this is not your fault."

Brad, who knew how sometimes Lizzy took things to heart that she shouldn't, wrapped his arms around her. His hands were still wet from the dirty dishwater but no one cared. She needed that hug more than she needed to be dry. He promised her that he was there and that God would work this all out.

Standing there in that moment, with the little baby in between them, she had a memory come back to her when their oldest son Garrett was a baby. She had a bad case of the baby blues. She couldn't snap out of the funk. She felt too young to be a mom, and they didn't have enough money. She felt tired all the time and inadequate, desperate. But, every night Brad would come home from work and wrap his strong arms around her and Garrett and he would pray for them.

"Honey, do you remember this?" she asked.

Automatically, he knew just what she was talking about. "Sure do, hon."

Both of their minds wandered back to that season in their life. And suddenly, the woman's decision to dine and dash made a lot more sense. What if Lizzy had not had Brad to walk with her through those times? What if they had no money or home? Or even a way to put a clean diaper on their baby? No wonder that woman did what she had done.

She hoped the woman was all right, but right now, the only thing she could do was to love on this little baby. Angel began stirring. She had only been asleep for about twenty minutes, but her little lips were moving incessantly, as if they were searching for food. She woke with a startle and began crying. Lizzy knew the baby was hungry.

"Do we have anything to feed her?" she asked Karlene.

"Well, I'm not sure if she is old enough to feed her applesauce," Karlene replied.

"Hey, how about if I run to the Wal-mart on the edge of town. I mean, I always said I would never shop on a holiday but, I think this is an exception," Brad said. "You can try to feed Angel some applesauce, but I'll get some formula and some bottle and maybe a couple more sleepers and diapers, maybe wipes. What about a binkie?"

"Brad, honey. We just need some food for this teeny, tiny little thing. I love your enthusiasm, but how fast do you think you can get there and get back?" Lizzy asked, bemused with her husband.

"In a jiffy," Brad said as he was walking out the door.

"As I said before, you have yourself a good one there." Karlene repeated.

Lizzy nodded. No matter what they had gone through in the past, she truly had found herself a good one.

They tried feeding the baby applesauce, but they decided against it. The poor baby girl was so weak that she could hardly hold her head up. They were afraid to try the solid food out of fear that the swallowing may be too much for her and she may choke.

So, Lizzy washed her hands with soap and water and rinsed three extra times, and then just let the baby gnaw at her pointer finger. For the moment that soothed the baby. She continued to walk around the kitchen, praying, rocking, swaying and speaking in soothing tones to the little baby girl. Before long, she was asleep again. She hoped that Brad would be back with food soon. She was realizing how weak this baby was and just how desperate need for food.

She checked the time. It was already 2:00 p.m. She wondered if they would be able to make dinner at Monica's. Probably not. But, at the thought of Monica, Lizzy had an idea.

Brad was not kidding when he said he would return in a jiffy. He was back in twenty-five minutes.

As soon as she saw him, she ran up to him and said, "Brad, I just had a thought." He nodded. He knew exactly what she was going to say.

"Jenny?"

"How did you know?" she asked.

"I just know how your mind works," he said with a smile. Then, he cautiously reminded her, "Honey, we are not in control in this situation. We do not know how these things work. There's a lot that we don't know."

She knew he was right. But, she still couldn't help but let herself dream.

Brad washed the bottles and got the formula mixed up. After all these years, he was still a pro. She gently woke the sleeping baby by putting the nipple of the bottle in her mouth. When the baby realized that food was there, she began to drink fast, in big baby gulps. She drank four ounces quicker than Lizzy thought was possible for an adult to drink from a cup. She asked Brad if he would make some more. This time he made six ounces. She drank about four of them and began to slow down. She seemed less ravenous and began to look more calm. Just as Lizzy pulled the second bottle out of her mouth, she saw a very official woman walk through the doors.

"Hi, my name is Missy. I'm here with children and youth. Let's talk about what happened today."

"I'm sorry, but did you just say your name was Missy?" Lizzy asked incredulously.

"Yes. Is there something wrong, ma'am?"

"No. Nothing's wrong. I just think you may know my friends." Lizzy responded.

The woman took a good long look at Lizzy. "Ma'am, before we are to go any farther, I need to make sure you did not say anything to the mother of this baby about any friends, did you?" Missy seemed very concerned.

"No, nothing, ma'am. I was just trying to help the mother out by changing the baby's diaper and holding her while the mom ate her meal. When I came out once the baby was cleaned up, she was gone."

Lizzy explained.

Looking for just a little more reassurance the social worker asked, "Was there anything else that you said? Anything that could have been deemed as coercion to leave the baby with you? Anything about you? Or friends? Are you 100 percent sure?"

"Yes, I'm sure." Lizzy kept nodding her head at the lady, hoping to send belief into her brain.

"I'm so glad to hear that," Missy said. "Good job. And thank you."

So, Missy and Lizzy reviewed the events of the day several times. Missy asked about the baby's general demeanor. "Did she seem to have been harmed in any way?"

"No, she didn't seem hurt. I'm not sure if she was neglected or if the mom was just doing the best she could with what she had." Lizzy then went on to explain the infection in the crease of the baby's neck and her horrible, raw diaper rash. She talked about the foul smell the baby carried with her.

"Well, given what little we know about the mom, she was most likely trying her best with what she had. It is still unacceptable for this little baby, but chances are the mom is living on the streets. It's a wonder this baby is still alive."

Lizzy looked down at the precious little miracle in her arms right now. "Thank you, Lord, for protecting her," she whispered.

"What else did the mom tell you about the baby? Any details? Anything at all?" Missy inquired.

"She only said, "Her name is Angel and she is seven months.""

Missy did the math backwards in her head. "That means she would have been born in April. I will call the hospitals in the area and see if there is a baby girl with that name born in April. Just for good measure, I'll have them check March and May too. That may help us locate the mother."

Lizzy was feeling her maternal heart stir up a bit. "Is this baby going back with the mother who abandoned her?"

Missy, understanding the emotion behind Lizzy's question, reached over and touched her shoulder. "Ma'am, sometimes, yes, depending on the situation and the details, sometimes babies like this do stay with their biological parents. But, sometimes, they are placed in new homes that can provide love and material needs for the baby. We will just see how this pans out, okay?"

Lizzy had tears in her eyes. She had hopes for this little Angel.

Quietly, Missy whispered, "You are Jenny's friend, aren't you? I remember pictures of you on her wall. They are my first pick for this baby's placement, if I have my way, okay?"

Lizzy nodded. She smiled, not just because the lady was thinking about Jenny and Ryan, but because of the pictures hanging in the living room at Jenny's. They had just taken new Bible study pictures over the summer. It had been a yearly tradition for the last three years. Each year she and Brad would host a daylong picnic for the Bible study group. It would start around 11:00 a.m. and last into the dark hours of the night. Those summer picnics with all their families were always so much fun. Husbands, kids, water balloon tosses, horseshoes, and swimming in the pool out back, and, of course, their picture.

The first year it had just been Lizzy, Jenny, and Monica. The next year, they added Kate to the mix. Now, they had Blair as part of their Bible study family. She looked down at the sleeping bundle in her arms. She thought of Kate's growing belly. Their family was growing in all kinds of ways.

While Lizzy was off in her daydream, the police officer showed up. She did not have to do quite as much talking this time, as Missy filled him in on most of the details. The police said they would do the best to find the mom, but in situations like this, it was nearly impossible. Missy shared the idea of calling the local hospitals and the police said they would take care of that. They had a whole team of people to research things like that, so that Missy could take care of her job. Missy looked grateful.

They worked through some logistics and then made the phone calls to have the baby placed with a foster care home.

"I don't understand?" Lizzy inquired.

"Since it is a holiday and no courts are open today, the baby must be placed in a court approved respite home. The county does not open back up until Monday morning. So, this little one will go to a home who is used to children coming and going like this. They will take very good care of her. They are trained to help a child be re-nourished once again quickly, and they are very loving people. I've worked with them for years."

Neither one of them made mention of Jenny, but she was on both of their minds.

Missy said, "I'll make some other phone calls too. Okay?"

Lizzy nodded, unsure of what she meant by that, but she was learning more and more that Missy had a real passion for what she did here. She just trusted that whatever she meant by that was okay.

Lizzy had grown quite accustomed to having the little baby nestled in the crook of her arms. For a seven-month-old baby, she was so tiny and her weight was not much more than a newborn, so she did not feel heavy, even after a couple hours being held.

Missy reached over to take the baby and get her put in a car seat carrier she had brought to transport her. Lizzy was hesitant.

"It's okay. I know this is hard." Missy reassured her.

Lizzy had tears dropping out of her eyes for the third time today. "Do you mind if I pray for her first?"

Missy looked a little surprised, but said, "Go right ahead."

So, Brad came over and the two of them prayed a little prayer over Baby Angel and sent her on her way with Missy.

Karlene came over and gave Lizzy a big hug. "I know this was a rough way to spend your Thanksgiving. But, God needed you here today. That little baby needed to rest in your arms and be prayed over. Thank you for giving your time today."

Brad looked down at his watch.

"It's 4:57. We will be late, but do you want to go to Monica's still?"

"Please." That was the only word Lizzy could muster out of her mouth.

28

Jenny loved the hustle and bustle of a household of people. Altogether, there were twenty-seven people at their house for Thanksgiving. The energy of the children was delightful. They had set games up in the living room, Connect Four, Sorry, and Memory Match. And the TV was on. Earlier everyone had enjoyed the parade, but one of Ryan's brothers had switched it over to football later in the day.

Dinner had been over for about an hour. Jenny had slipped out to the porch just for a moment of fresh air and time alone with the Lord. She thanked God for their family: how God had brought Ryan's mom back to walking with him, how they had lots of nieces and nephews to spoil, how both her grandparents and Ryan's grandma were still here to celebrate the holidays with them. It was all such a blessing. She prayed for each person under her roof, and then she prayed for her other family that was not with them today, her Bible study family. They were like a little oddball group of sisters. And, she thanked God for the brilliant sun, shining, even though it was cold and windy. While she was breathing in another deep breath of crisp air, she heard the phone ring.

Ryan opened up the back door, and joined her on the porch to get away from the noise inside.

"Oh my goodness. Are you kidding me? Okay, we will not. We will. Thank you. Good-bye. Yes, you too. Happy Thanksgivng. Thank you so much."

"Who was that? It sounded important. Is everything okay?" Jenny blurted out as soon as the phone call had ended.

"Jenny, that was Missy. She said she might have a baby in mind for us. She wanted to call and share the news with us on Thanksgiving. The baby is seven months old. She's in a respite home right now. But, pending the search for the mom, they may need a home for this baby. She said she would call us with more information on Monday when she returned for the holiday. She also said to not get our hopes up, but depending on the search for the parents, the baby could be placed with us soon."

Jenny started jumping frantically up and down.

"We are going to be parents! It's happening! It's happening so fast!"

"Jenny, calm down, honey. She said to make sure that we didn't get our hopes up too high. Okay? There's a lot that could happen, okay."

Jenny hated to have her spirits dampened, but she knew he was right.

"Oh, do you want to know the weirdest part?" Ryan asked.

"What?"

"Missy said that one of our friends was in charge of the baby." Ryan was puzzled. I don't know who it was, but she said they were at the shelter working this morning.

"Oh my goodness! It was Lizzy! Lizzy was there today!" Jenny was excited all over again.

Ryan decided just to let her bask in the excitement. Yes, there was a lot that could happen, but sometimes, you just needed to be happy.

"Ryan, what time is it?"

He looked at his watch. "It's after six"

"She should be at Monica's by now. I'm calling."

"Hon, it's Thanksgiving. Can you wait until tomorrow?"

"Not when it comes to our new baby!" Jenny said excitedly.

Ryan handed the phone over to her, and was in awe at just how fast his wife's fingers could dial when they were excited.

"Monica, is she there? Is Lizzy there?" she practically hollered into the phone.

"Yeah, hold on a sec." Monica called for Lizzy. "Lizzy, Jenny is on the phone for you. She sounds crazy!"

Monica had no idea what was going on. Lizzy had committed herself to being quiet about it, not wanting to overstep any bounds.

When Jenny explained that Missy had called, Lizzy shared a little bit of what had happened that day. She did not tell Jenny how beautiful the baby was, or how hard it was to hand the baby over to Missy. She just told her what had happened at the shelter.

Jenny kept begging for more details, but Lizzy didn't really have a whole lot of other information to share. She just assured Jenny that she was praying for that baby and she hoped and prayed passionately that the baby would indeed end up with Ryan and Jenny.

Jenny realized after they hung up the phone that Lizzy had sounded a little worn out. She was so excited with her news that she had not even thought about what kind of day Lizzy must have had. Though she was strong, Lizzy was very sensitive, and things often took quite an emotional toll on her, whether she would let on to that fact or not.

Jenny looked at Ryan, hugged him, and said, "Can we just keep this to ourselves for today. Let's cherish it together, and praise God. Is that okay with you?"

Ryan said, "I'm glad you suggested it. Let's not get everyone else involved until we know more about what is going to happen."

They stood on the porch, both praying silently for a baby girl they now knew existed out there. They prayed she was okay. And that she was safe and that soon she would be theirs.

29

It was 5:00 a.m. on Friday, Black Friday, Her favorite Friday of the entire year. But, Blair woke up just cranky. She knew she needed an attitude check when she could wake up cranky after a day of praising God for everything good in her life.

But, it all came back to Carlee.

It had been almost a week since she had spoken to Carlee, and her friend should have at least received one or two of the cinnamon rolls and coffee by now. However, the phone had not rung as she had hoped it would.

Last year, on Black Friday, Carlee and Blair had spent the entire day together. They left their homes at 4:00 a.m. to stand in line to buy both of their husbands new GPSs and Carlee bought a new TV for their family room. They went out for breakfast, and then hit up some clothing sales, followed by going out for lunch. They then went to stores that were selling Christmas decorations at heavily discounted prices, and they hit a late day sale that started at 5:00 p.m. for bedding. They literally shopped until they dropped. They had so much fun dodging other shoppers, finding prime parking spots, laughing, chatting with other adventurous shoppers, and of course eating out all day long. Even though shopping was not the highlight of a normal day for Blair, on Black Friday, shopping turned her Plain Jane personality into a competitive athlete, who enjoyed the challenge and thrill of finding the deeply discounted deals. And it was a day with her best friend.

Now that Blair was reliving last year, she had begun to sink into a dangerous cave of self-pity. It was Black Friday, and, none of her new friends were really into that tradition. And, she didn't even have a best friend here now. She enjoyed the Bible study girls, but none of them were really her best friend. The relationship she had built with them was deep, but not deep enough to talk about marital troubles, or hormones, or money. Best friend things.

Not to mention that money was tighter here in Tennessee. While Samuels's job paid more than his last job, they were still paying on two houses, waiting for their other one to sell in North Carolina. They were very comfortable here, but not enough to go and blow several hundreds of dollars on a day of shopping.

Nevertheless, it was like her body woke up, ready to go. The one day in the entire year where her body was ready to wake up at 4:00 a.m. Being alert now for over an hour, her mood worsening by the minute, Blair went downstairs to make coffee. She tried talking to God, but was so ashamed when everything she said sounded like complaining. Just when she thought she had come so far, there she was, acting like the old Blair again. Shame filled her thoughts and she was embarrassed of how she was acting.

The more ashamed she was of herself, the more she tried shifting blame to Carlee. If Carlee would have just called me and apologized, if Carlee would have never yelled at me or hung up with me on the phone. if Carlee would just be happy for me and where I am in life . . . Excuse after excuse tried to sneak its way in and assure Blair that her bad attitude was okay.

But, the mom in her stirred. Or maybe it was the Holy Spirit. Either way Blair kept having the admonishment she often gave her children flow through her mind. "You are the only one responsible for your behavior. You cannot blame anyone else for the way you behave." Ouch.

Not even Carlee could be responsible for how she felt this morning. She was choosing to focus on what she was lacking—money for a shopping spree, a built in best friend, a phone call of apology, instead of focusing on what she did have: a house, a family, a group of friends, who consistently encouraged her, and a God who loved her despite her bad attitude.

One time in passing, Lizzy said at Bible study that the best way to leave your own pity party is to do something for someone else. Blair had spoken to Lizzy on the phone yesterday and knew that she and Ryan had a very long day, a very emotionally tiring day. Blair now knew she was called to serve others. Armed with that information, she surveyed the fridge and then sent a text. She knew Lizzy didn't turn her phone on until she was up and moving, so she didn't worry about waking her. The text said, "Breakfast at my place. 8:45 a.m."

Blair prayed, "God, help me serve others and you, and help me fling this bad attitude to the curb. And, even though it's hard for me to pray a blessing on her right now, please, be with Carlee today. I know she's out shopping. Keep her safe. Thanks, Lord." Even while she was praying, she had darts of anger spring up at Carlee, but she kept handing the thoughts over one by one.

Blair got to work. She pulled down her big, thick, red binder of recipes. The first page was the messiest page. It was for sour cream pancakes, Samuel's favorite. She double-checked to make sure that she had all the ingredients and she did. She flipped the pages to find the quiche recipe that had been her favorite since they got married. Amazingly, they actually had all the ingredients for that recipe too.

She began cracking eggs, whipping them with cream, and shredding cheese. The oven was preheating. The veggies were being chopped. And the coffee aroma filled the kitchen with an extra layer of scent that added calmness to the morning preparations. Instead of focusing on the people she didn't have right now, she would serve those who were in her life. She would serve them with joy and a heart of praise, even if she had to ask God to redirect her thoughts a hundred times.

The quiche recipe needed about an hour to bake and a little time to set up after it was out of the oven, so she put it in the oven about 7:15. As she closed the oven door, her phone rang. It was Lizzy. "Oh, Blair, what a blessing you are! Ryan and I are so happy to come over this morning. Yesterday was a rough, emotional day. And while we are thankful for everything that has happened, we could use a little bit of Blair cooking that we have come to love! Between you and Monica,

Brad and I will have to start our New Year's resolution to lose weight a month early!"

Blair smiled. She was needed. And despite her attitude being up and down all morning, she knew that God was teaching her. She went and woke up her sleeping family around 8:00. Everyone was so excited to hear that Lizzy and Ryan were coming over.

Blair hopped in the shower and put on her Friday shirt, light blue. She found the matching hair tie. She looked in the mirror and was a little discouraged about how boring she felt, especially when she knew that Lizzy would be coming looking like a fashion plate. She brushed her hair and used the blow dryer just enough so that her hair would not make the shirt dotted with water droplets. She walked into her room and put on her socks. And, since it was a day to be spent at home, she grabbed her comfy brown slippers. The insides of them were toasty since they had been sitting right in front of the heater vent. She wiggled her toes and tried to spread the heat around to her entire foot. As she was soaking in the heat, the doorbell rang.

"Have I been in the shower that long?" she wondered out loud. She glanced at the clock, noting that it was only 8:21. "I guess Lizzy and Ryan are early." Carefully Blair descended the stairs, making sure not trip on her fuzzy, oversized footwear. Samuel had gotten to the door first, and Blair's stomach did a flip-flop when she heard the voice at the entryway say, "Hey, Sam! It's so good to see you! Is Blair home?"

Forgetting the concern for safety, Blair skipped down the last three steps faster than she should. She hit the foyer floor, skidded right to the door and wrapped her arms around the guest waiting there for her. "Carlee, I can't believe it's you! You are here!"

Carlee smiled, but there were tears in her eyes. She looked down at the ground, and had a difficult time actually looking at Blair. "Blair, I just couldn't spend the day apart from you." Blair hugged her friend and said that she had been struggling all morning long too.

Carlee put her hand up, pausing Blair's part of the conversation. "It's more than that, Blair. I can't believe how awful I was to you on the phone. You are the one who has been uprooted, who is trying to build a life here. I know that takes time. And, then, then, you sent those let-

156

ters." Carlee's voice was shaky and emotional. "You bought me coffee even though you are so far away. The first day, I was so mad at you. If it hadn't been my favorite, I would have thrown it away. But, by the third day, it just made me think about how sweet you are, even when I'm awful. I'm so sorry."

Blair replied, "It's tough on all of us. And you've been forgiven. Even though I was struggling, wondering why I hadn't heard from you yet. But, this is better than any phone call!"

As they hugged another couple of times, and Blair brought Carlee in and showed her around their new home, a moment of panic struck her. Lizzy was on her way over. How would Carlee react to that? She took a deep breath and mentioned the impending breakfast to her friend.

Carlee's face did take on a bit of sadness as she thought about sharing her old friend with her new friends. But, she said, "I'm here, in your world right now. I want to see what your new world is all about, and who is in your life nowadays."

Blair hugged her and reassured Carlee that she would love Lizzy.

Blair could not have been more accurate in that prediction. When Lizzy arrived, she wrapped her arms around Carlee in a big Lizzy style hug. "Oh, girl! Blair has talked so much about you. I feel like I already know you!"

The children were so excited to see Carlee again, and the conversation at breakfast was light hearted and fun. Samuel, knowing what a treat this was for Blair, offered to clean up the breakfast mess while the ladies enjoyed coffee and more chitchat. Ryan happily agreed to help Samuel, and the ladies went off to the comfort of the living room.

As they walked to the room Carlee giggled. "Oh, Blair, you make me laugh. Even with this big, new fancy house, all the rooms are painted tan. You really love the simple things, don't you?"

Blair laughed. "I guess. Although, I really broke out of my shell, and painted the downstairs bathroom blue."

"Wow! You *are* growing," her friend teased.

Blair ended up being an observer for much of the conversation between Lizzy and Carlee. They loved getting to know one another, and Blair felt her heart ease as Carlee really seemed to enjoy interacting with someone from her new life. The pressure was diminishing moment by moment and she could feel relaxation overtake her. Here she was with two very different friends, from two very different times in her life, and they were meshing.

As she observed this taking place, it was almost as if she felt like she was becoming more and more complete like there was no longer and old Blair and a new Blair but just a Blair who was growing, changing, and allowing herself to be molded. She enjoyed the way it sounded, hearing her two friends voices ping pong back and forth. The way they compared notes on her behavior, how they both spoke kindly of her, and how they appreciated her simplicity, and her joy in the little things, like matching a ponytail holder with a t-shirt. Blair felt like she could listen to them chat all day.

However, that plan was interrupted by the ringing of the telephone. "Hey Blair, I think you need to take this phone call, hon," Samuel called from the kitchen. "It's Monica. She's crying or something."

Lizzy hopped up and followed Blair. Following suit, Carlee also went into the kitchen.

"Monica, are you okay? What's going on?" They all waited for a response.

"Oh my gracious! Are you kidding?" She nodded, with a shocked look on her face and then yelled out, "Oh wow!"

It was very difficult for the bystanders to get a feel of what the conversation was about.

"What's going on?" Lizzy demanded. Blair waved her off, still intently listening to the phone line, trying to make sense of what she was hearing.

"Yes, okay. Yeah, she's here. That's why you couldn't reach her at her house. Do you want to tell her?" Another pause. "Okay, I will." More pause. "Okay, sounds great!"

She hung up the phone. She smiled and took a deep breath. "Wow. This is turning out to be quite a day, and it's not even noon yet!"

"What in the world is going on? I cannot figure out if I'm sending congratulations or condolences," Lizzy responded, quite puzzled.

Blair smiled. "Trust me, it's great. But, I cannot tell you."

Blair turned and looked at Carlee. "Would you like to see a little bit more of the neighborhood and meet a couple other friends?"

Carlee smiled. "I would love to."

"Samuel, Ryan, do you guys mind if we take a little field trip?" Samuel looked a little inquisitive and Blair whispered a secret message into his ear. He smiled at Lizzy and said he'd be happy to entertain Ryan with Sports Center and left over pie while they went on a little errand.

Blair took her slippers off, and placed them once again by the heater and switched to her boots. They all put on their hats, gloves, and coats and headed to Blair's car. As they shivered, Blair wondered if maybe she should have warmed up the car before they climbed in. Through chattering teeth, Lizzy begged once more to know what was going on, or at least where they were going. Blair giggled at the fun of the secret. "You'll know soon enough."

As they drove through the neighborhood, Blair pointed out their post office, the kid's school, and the local grocery store. She knew they were not that interesting of landmarks to Carlee, but she needed something else to chat about, so she would not give away the secret.

However, Monica's face did not have the ability to hold any secret. As soon as they pulled into Monica's parent's driveway, she opened the front door. Even through the foggy car windows, her huge smile was evident. Jer and Mandy were standing in the doorway as well. Lizzy hopped out of the car as soon as it was stopped. "No way!" she yelled as she ran up and embraced all three of them at one time.

In new fiancée fashion, Monica held out her left hand. It was sparkling with a simple round cut diamond. While the ring was not particularly large, you could tell that Monica was thrilled with the presence of it on her finger. Little Mandy was beaming. In her sweet little voice she proclaimed, "My other dad may have gone to Heaven, but God knew I needed one here on earth." Mandy then showed a ring on her finger too. "Jer asked me if I wanted him to be my daddy. I said yes. And he gave me this pretty ring."

Her little blue eyes sparkled. Blair's heart warmed as she peered at Mandy's tiny left ring finger. It had a gold band with a pretty pink heart stone on the top. Mandy looked just as happy as her mom did.

Blair hugged them, and then she reached back and grabbed Carlee's hand. "Guys, I'm so excited for you! And I'm excited for you to meet my friend, Carlee, too!"

Monica, so overcome with happiness, just hopped down the couple of steps and wrapped her arms around Carlee. Mandy followed suit. Jer laughed and then shook Carlee's hand.

It was just a few minutes later when Jenny and Kate arrived in Kate's vehicle. More hugs, squeals, and gazes at the rings occurred. Finally, Jer broke the girly party up with his deep manly voice, "So, do you ladies think we could move this celebration inside? It's pretty cold out here!"

They all quickly filed inside, and headed right to the family room. Monica's dad had the fireplace warmed up with a crackling fire and her mom was waiting with cups of cocoa and cookies. They obviously were thrilled by the news and Monica's mom often stopped and looked at her daughter's happy face. Just like a group of teenagers, they sat criss-crossed in front of the fire, in a circle. Jer, however, decided to position himself in the recliner. He joked and said, "I guess I knew when I proposed that it was a package deal."

Once again, Carlee seemed to fit right in with her new friends. And Mandy took a particular liking to Carlee. Kids always did gravitate towards her. Mandy plopped her little body right in the middle of Carlee's lap. "I'm glad for a new friend," Mandy sweetly proclaimed.

Carlee smiled and looked at Blair. "Me too," she said quietly.

Even though Thanksgiving was officially over, the thankfulness celebrated the day before spilled over into Blair's heart that day too. It was one of the richest moments of her year so far. It was not every day that you got to celebrate with all your closest friends, especially, engagements, babies and forgiveness. Her heart was overcome with happiness. Just as earlier, Carlee's voice flowed naturally in conversation and it seemed like they had all always been together. The happiness of the moment overtook her and the next thing she knew, she had tears just flowing down her eyes.

Kate, noticing the tears asked gently, "Blair, are you okay?"

Blair smiled, and said, "I do not think I have ever been better."

30

Lizzy woke up, hopped out of bed with an excited feeling. It was Tuesday finally. It had felt like ages since they had all sat together in Monica's comfy family room. Their little worlds had changed so much in just a week. Even though her weekend had been rich with fellowship, she had not spent a lot of time in God's word. She imagined the rest of the girls had found themselves struggling with the same issue. Everyone had been so busy with the holiday and big changes and often, at least in her own life, that quiet time with God was the first thing to disappear. It was so needed for her today. And it had been a long time since she felt like she could share the Word of God so passionately from her heart, so sincerely. Often, when she was teaching from the Bible, she felt like a failure, almost hypocritical. She felt short most of the time. But today, she was excited. She had lived this verse out at the shelter the other day. And while she didn't always do things perfectly, it felt good to actually have a verse that she had at least kind of lived out the right way recently. They were studying the verse that said, "Live in harmony with each other. Don't be too proud to enjoy the company of ordinary people. And don't think you know it all!" Thoughts of last Thursday, how serving what Jesus would have called the least of these, crossed her mind. Even though the day itself had been hard, she was so excited to share with the ladies about her experiences. She had felt so at ease with the people there, even with Baby Angel's mom, before she left anyways. The other workers had shared during the prep time that morning how you would learn so much from the people you were serving. And even though the baby's situation took up most of her time that day, she knew that God had changed her heart forever. She felt so alive and was excited to go back and work at the shelter soon. She realized that the people who they were serving at the shelter were simply just ordinary people. And she wanted to spend more time them.

As the member of their group all arrived, everyone was talking up a storm. "And then Missy called me back. Legally, they have to do their best to search for the mom, and while they are doing that the baby will stay in respite care. All our paperwork has gone through, and we are ready to go, so if they cannot find the mom, or the mom signs off, she can be placed with us, maybe even before Christmas. However, she will be placed with us as a foster to adopt case, which means the finalization may be longer." Jenny was so excited about everything happening in their world. Lizzy worried about Jenny's heart, which had a tendency to be very tender. Lizzy tried not to let her mind wander to all the ways this situation may not work out, but it kept going there. She needed to have faith right now for Jenny and for Baby Angel.

The conversation paused for just a minute and then more questions came. "When did Carlee leave to go home?"

"So, have you and Jer talked about dates yet?"

"How are you feeling, Kate? Do you feel more energetic yet? What did the boys say when you told them?"

"Carlee had to leave Friday night. She got home safely. She texted me when she got home."

"We have some dates in mind."

"I'm still really tired, but it helps to know why. The boys are bouncing off the walls"

After the social recap had finished, and they had prayed for the situations in their lives, Lizzy shared the scripture verse. She even surprised herself as the passion for the shelter poured out. They had a very open and honest discussion.

Lizzy asked, "Have you ever felt like you were better than someone else?"

Kate was quick to respond. "No, but I always felt like people thought they were better than me and Phil. Everyone knew we fought a lot. And since we didn't get Christianized or whatever until we were adults, we had a lot to overcome to fit in with the churchy crowd."

Lizzy responded, "I love the word Christianized."

Kate laughed. "Yeah, but you know what I mean"

Monica took a breath and very gently asked Kate, "So, do you think people really thought that?"

Kate said, "Looking back, no. At the time, I think I felt inferior, so I automatically assumed everyone else thought I was. Now, in retrospect, I see people were just trying to help us."

Monica nodded. "Do you know, I found the same thing to be true? For the first few years when Deke left me, I felt like everyone judged me for being a single mom, and for being divorced. In reality, the only one who ever judged me, that I know of for sure, anyways, was myself."

The room quieted with thought and then Blair spoke up, "I have."

She took another deep breath. "I have thought I was better than someone before."

Lizzy asked, "Are you okay with sharing about it?"

"Kay, I will. When we lived in North Carolina, our neighbor, not Carlee, but our other neighbor, had two boys. And her boys were mischievous. And I always just told myself I was a better mom than her. But, I realize that my kids are all just really good natured. Maybe she was a good mom, but she has two hard-to-raise kids."

Lizzy nodded. It was an uncomfortable silence, but then Jenny said, "Even though I'm not a mom yet, I actually have done that before too. I remember seeing a mom in the grocery store and thinking in my mind that I would be a much better mom than that."

Monica smiled. "I'll never forget this time when Mandy was three. We were grocery shopping. For some reason she hadn't got her nap that day and the child was determined she was getting M&M's. Now, you all know how I feel about M&M's, so I told her no candy. She threw a fit. Many people stared at us as she screamed. One young lady shook her head at me, obviously disgusted with my parenting skills.

But, another woman, she was older, and really sweet, she came to me and said, "Honey, if they are screaming like that, it means you are sticking to your guns. You're raising that baby girl right." That woman was living that verse out to me. She was not thinking she was better than me. She was encouraging me. She was associating with me, even though she didn't have to."

"Wow! What a great example, Monica," Lizzy stated. "Maybe we could all look for little ways to encourage other moms, other women like that."

Everyone in the group nodded, realizing just how applicable these verses were in everyday living.

31

"Mama, when you marry Jer, we are going to have to stop eating fruit for dessert you know." Mandy was serious, and a little worried.

"Why do you say that honey girl?" Monica inquired.

"Well, have you ever noticed that sometimes fruit doesn't taste the same as chocolate?"

"Yeah, sweetie. That's because it's not."

Mandy giggled. "I know that Mama, but Jer doesn't eat fruit when it's time for dessert. He told me one time that sometimes he just wants to eat real sugar when it's dessert time. Not just bananas."

"Well, honey, he said sometimes. I know Jer loves pies and chocolate cake, and we can make that on the weekends for him, as a special treat. He's been a single man for a long time. But, don't you worry. Jer and I've talked about all kinds of stuff, even about fruit for dessert. He's still excited to be part of our family, even if we ate fruit for dessert every night."

Grabbing her chapter book that she needed to read for school, Mandy curled up next to Monica. Monica giggled inwardly and shook her head. That man did love his sugar. She remembered him commenting on their healthy eating habits very early on, when they had just been emailing back and forth.

"I guess if we ever get married, I will have to clean up some of my eating habits, huh?" he had written. Never in a million years would Monica have guessed that indeed, she would be the one marrying him, helping him grow accustomed to veggies at every meal and fruit or tea to finish supper.

The thought about sharing a meal with him every night made a twinge of excitement run up her spine. "Mandy, things will be very different. But, I really think, when we get all adjusted, that we will be very happy."

"Mama, I really believe that too." She smiled at her mom, and continued reading.

Most of the time, Monica focused her thoughts on the very practical side of the engagement. They were studying with her pastor for pre-marital counseling. Jer was very determined to do things the right way, especially considering Mandy was in the mix. There were so many big decisions to make. The first one was when to get married. They had decided that the end of January would be a great time. It was a slow time of year for most of their family and friends and would be great to break up the monotony of winter every year with an anniversary celebration. Then, the biggest decision after that was where to live. Jer had a very nice apartment, and it was actually pretty roomy, with 3 bedrooms. However, it was not in Mandy's school district and they did not want to move Mandy out of there if they did not have to. They both quickly agreed that starting a new life in a new place together would be absolutely amazing. The house hunt was on.

They had spent an entire Saturday with a realtor visiting all the houses for sale in the school district that Mandy attended. Some of the homes were much too extravagant for their taste, not to mention their budget. And a few houses were a little too run down to even consider, seeing that they planned on enjoying their first years together, and not spending them remodeling a house in disarray. But, there were three homes that were just what they were looking for. They had deliberated over them for weeks. Each home had three bedrooms and was similar in square footage. But, Monica had been drawn to the home that had a beautiful flower and herb garden in the back. Even though the winter dismal gray sky and left over frost damage had made the garden look sad and weepy, Monica could imagine the joy and life that sprang from the garden spring and summertime. She could imagine the life in the garden and in the home.

She loved dreaming about what it would be like to sit with Jer and Mandy in the mornings, reading from the Bible, on the back patio overlooking the gardens. Maybe they would even sing worship songs quietly, so as not to disturb the neighbors.

The kitchen at their new home was not big, but it was comfortable, with a small island that would be just big enough for the three of them to sit around. Monica and Mandy loved baking cookies on December evenings when the winter chill would come around. She would let her mind imagine what it would be like sipping hot cocoa, enjoying those cookies together. Maybe Jer might give her a quick kiss and whisper that he loved her in her ear, and how she could cherish moments like that often with her little family. It would be different, much different that life was currently. Now, even though they loved baking cookies, they were doing it in her mom's home. She could never let the dishes wait until after the cookies had been enjoyed, and she sometimes worried about replacing the ingredients she had used right away so that she would not mess up her mom's menu plans. Even though she had been grateful for the time her parents had invested in her life, she dreamed of doing life in her own way, finding her own person. Deke had controlled her, demanded that she did things his way. Her parents, while always sweet, still were her parents. She had lived in their house, with their rules.

Here she was, on the brink of starting a brand-new life, with a man who had been so wonderful to her, in their very own home. As the excitement worked its way through her body, she pulled Mandy up off the couch, and the two of them began jumping up and down.

32

"I'm not sure I have ever felt like I had an enemy before. But, now, I feel like I'm surrounded by them," Kate said sadly at their next Bible study meeting. "At least God knew that I needed to hear this verse today, right?"

Lizzy nodded her head, remembering the time in her life when she felt like the enemy in her life was her very own husband. She had prayed about this Bible study a lot. It was a rough topic, one that she had struggled with in various aspects of her life, from time to time. Sometimes she wondered how anyone could even imagine having an enemy.

Kate began to share the story of a teacher who really seemed to have it out for Jeff. She was near tears, as she shared how Jeff's home-room teacher had been so impressed with his behavior lately. Kate smiled as she thought about the extra time that Phil had been spending with him, and how his involvement was no doubt the catalyst to the positive change.

Kate talked about how they switched classes for social studies and health. The social studies teacher had sent home notes day after day about how Jeff was behaving. Kate was puzzled. She was used to getting notes about Jeff and his high energy levels being disruptive. She had even dealt with him fighting with other students. But, these notes suggested it was more than being disruptive, and his disagreement was with the teacher, and not another student. Despite all his shortcomings, Jeff had never been outright disrespectful to a teacher before. She stated he was being rude, snarky, and at times down right disobedient.

Kate had made an appointment to talk with the teacher, who could not find one reinforcing thing to say about Jeff. Kate asked if there were any suggestions on how to get the boy to fit into the classroom setting better, or if there was any particular reason she felt he was struggling so badly there. The teacher just curtly replied, "I have no idea what is going on with your child, but you better figure it out." Kate had never heard a teacher so curt. It left her stunned. She really had no clue what to do.

She talked to Phil later that evening and they had called Jeff into their room. "Son, what in the world is going on?" Phil asked. Kate knew he was trying to be gentle, but his voice sounded exasperated and rough.

"Dad, I just gave up. She hates me. That teacher makes me feel dumb. I don't wanna listen to her. She's a mean, old lady. She makes me mad."

"Son, no matter how she treats you, she is your teacher. She's a grown-up. You need to respect her," Phil responded, this time a little softer.

"Dad, why do I hafta respect someone who ain't respecting me?" Jeff demanded.

The room fell silent and Phil directed his son to brush his teeth. "Your mom and I will talk and pray about this more. We'll figure out how to help you."

Kate had prayed that Phil's promise for a solution was not an empty one.

She said, "Ladies, I really do feel like this teacher has it out for my son. I know he can be a handful, but he's really trying. Does anyone have any insight for me?"

Lizzy said, "Well, what if we really prayed about you and Jeff and Phil applying this verse directly to this situation. We can all brainstorm together. Do you think Jeff would go along with it? Do you think Phil would be willing to try it?"

Kate nodded. "Phil is so on fire for the Lord right now that I think he would do anything that God's word says. Now, Jeff may be harder to convince, since he's the one living this, but I think, Lizzy, if you encouraged him he may. He just adores you. Whatcha got in mind girls?'

No one said anything for a few minutes. Then Blair spoke up, "What about an apology note from Jeff. You know, just for being disobedient."

They all nodded.

Jenny spoke up. "You are not gonna like my suggestion, but what about giving her a gift?"

Kate shrugged her shoulders.

"You know, feed her or give her something to drink, just like verse 20 says. Maybe a Starbucks card?"

"Wow," Kate said that word, in amazement. She felt the baby kick then. She put her hand on her growing baby bump and nodded. The baby's kick was a reminder to her that they were trying to live a new life, do things God's way. "Okay, I'll give it a shot," she said.

They prayed for the teacher again, and then they spent time slowly reading the passage of Scripture for the week.

Never pay back evil with more evil. Do things in such a way that everyone can see you are honorable.

Dear friends, never take revenge. Leave that to the righteous anger of God. For the Scriptures say;

"I will take revenge; I will pay them back," says the LORD. Instead, "If your enemies are hungry, feed them. If they are thirsty, give them something to drink. In doing this, you will heap burning coals of shame on their heads." Don't let evil conquer you, but conquer evil by doing good

They also prayed for Jeff. What an energetic little man he was. They prayed that he would be open to trying something new for the Lord. As they wrapped up Bible study that day, Lizzy said she had a few announcements to make.

"Ladies, I just want to say that I think this is perhaps the most life changing Bible study that I have ever done before. What a crazy four months it has been. I can't believe the enormous changes that have taken place in our lives. Blair, you have been an incredible addition to our little Bible study family. You and your family are just beautiful. Our family is growing through marriage, babies, and through friendships. It's amazing. However, I think with the Christmas season, we may need to take a hiatus. I'm thinking until May."

"May? Lizzy? That's a long time!" Jenny interjected.

Lizzy, ever so maternal and kind reached over and patted Jenny's hand. "Jenny, we have a wedding to help with. And if we have our way, you will be getting Baby Angel any day now. I think even though we will not be having our weekly Bible study for a few months that we will see each other more than normal. Kate will be having her baby in that time frame, and Monica is going to need time to adjust in her new home, with her new husband. There's a lot going on and we need to give ourselves time to adjust."

Sadly, the Bible study members saw Lizzy's point. They were all very busy right now. And, truthfully, they all saw each other at least once, if not two or three times outside of Bible study. But, nothing, simply nothing came close to this amazing time of study. Hesitantly, the group decided that perhaps a hiatus would be okay.

33

Lizzy was not a fan of being on hiatus from the Bible study. However, she knew she had done what was best for the group. The hectic pace of life had picked up even though a harsh winter tried its best to slow their Tennessee community down. The Bible study has been one that needed time to sink in deep in their hearts anyways. The group had promised to read Romans 12 at least once a week. Lizzy had found that by now she had most of the twenty-one verses memorized as it was. With the harsh winter, and a little extra time off during the week, Lizzy had started spending most Wednesday afternoons at the soup kitchen. While the crowds did not compare with Thanksgiving, there often was still a sizeable group for lunch on the days the kitchen was open. Lizzy had really come to love the regulars she saw each week. The harsh odors and foul language did not bother her quite as much now, especially as she began to learn names and stories. Sometimes the opportunity arose where she could pray for someone, or even hug them. Before serving here, Lizzy had never thought about how few hugs a homeless person received. Those hugs were cherished more than currency of any kind.

Lizzy was busy tidying up the dessert table, which had moments ago been piled high with chocolate chip cookies and peanut butter blossoms. Suddenly she felt someone grab her arm. She felt her arm twisting behind her, and whoever had her arm was trying to push her down to the ground. "Owwww, please stop!" Lizzy yelled out loud.

Hearing Lizzy's cry for help, Karlene looked out the window from the kitchen. "Oh no!" Karlene muttered. She grabbed the phone, dialed 911, and then tried to come to Lizzy's rescue.

Lizzy's attacker had finally succeeded in getting her to the ground. Lizzy felt something hard hitting her head. "Where did you take my baby? Where did you take her?" Lizzy was able to look up and see a silver colored metal ladle coming down again, on her forehead. Her assailant was baby Angel's mother. Karlene did her best to get the scoop out of the attacker's hand.

"Please, stop hurting her." Karlene begged. Other patrons of the soup kitchen were stunned. No one seemed to know what to do. Thankfully, it was less than three minutes before the police arrived. They immediately took baby Angel's mother into custody, and upon assessing Lizzy's condition, decided that an ambulance should be called.

The rest of the day seemed to go by in a blur. As Lizzy was being treated in the emergency room, the police had contacted Baby Angel's caseworker. Missy had immediately called Jenny.

"Jenny, I'm sorry. With the assault on your friend, the baby will not be placed with you. The risk is too high. Please, understand that this is no one's fault. There will be a baby out there for you. Angel is just not that baby. We will be placing her with another family as soon as her mother is officially identified and charged."

Jenny was confused. "What do you mean an assault on my friend?" As Missy explained the story, Jenny crumpled on the floor and wept. "She attacked Lizzy? Oh, oh my. Oh, no!" Jenny cried out.

Missy explained that she had to go and tend to more legal details concerning the baby. She wished her the best of luck with her friend, and once again assured her that someday they would end up with a baby. As the phone call ended Jenny wondered how this could be happening. They had prayed for that baby every day since Thanksgiving. They believed that she was theirs. Not only was the baby ripped from their hands, but just days before Christmas their sweet friend, Lizzy, was lying in a hospital after being brutally attacked. Her dream had quite literally turned to a nightmare. She called Ryan, who was leaving work to come be with her. Then she decided that she better call the rest of the group and fill them in on the horrible events of the day.

As she dialed Monica's number, Jenny could barely speak through the sobs. After about ten minutes of coercing, Monica had somehow interpreted the main ideas of the phone call through Jenny's mournful wailing. Monica assured her that she would call the other two friends needing notified, and when the call was disconnected, Jenny reached for a pillow off of the couch and laid her head down and let every bit of pain that was in her heart out. She knew that this hurt was a new kind of pain in her soul, a mother's agony. The realization that a mother's heart was growing in her made the pain richer, deeper and more sorrowful.

Jenny was unsure of how much time had passed. When she realized that Ryan was kneeling over her, praying for her, she opened her eyes. The world felt darker, dimmer, and there was a general lack of hope. Ryan just kept running his fingers over her hair, rubbing her back, and giving her tender kisses, all the while wiping away his own tears, and praying for his own broken heart too. Neither of them knew how to move from this place. In fact, while the rest of the world continued on its busy way, Ryan and Jenny laid side by side, between the coffee table and the couch for the next seven hours, afraid that moving from that spot would stir up even more pain.

34

Over the course of the next several weeks, Lizzy healed from her physical attack with much more success than Jenny and Ryan recovered from their heartbreak. Despite a few lingering yellow spots left over from bruising, and three scars on her forehead where the ladle had cut her, Lizzy's body was returning to normal. The cast on her right arm was set to come off next Friday, the day before Jer and Monica's wedding. Throughout recovery, Lizzy had spent much time in prayer with Karlene, the director of the soup kitchen, praying for Baby Angel's mom. Upon her arrest, they had learned the mother's sordid history. She had been a prostitute, and also had several warrants out for her arrest for stealing, beating a woman in the street, and she was believed to be connected with a drug circle that was causing mayhem on the west side of their little town. Baby Angel had been placed in a home a few towns over, where she would be adopted and loved.

As often as they prayed for Baby Angel's mom, they lifted up Jenny and Ryan even more. Their hearts had been broken in pieces. "How could a loving God allow their hearts to be destroyed like that?" Jenny had asked that question several times and the only answers they had came straight from God's word. "Jenny, I don't know what God is doing, but he's got your best in mind. I know Romans 8:28 sounds trite right now, but He's working this out for your good." Lizzy would often remind her.

Jenny could barely look at Lizzy most of the time. While she knew it was irrational to be angry at Lizzy, she was the easiest target. If she had never gotten involved in this situation, then they would not have broken hearts right now. The distance caused by Jenny's anger made all the group gatherings awkward, and Jenny had actually stopped coming around whenever she could find a decent enough excuse.

No excuse would be good enough to skip tonight though. Tonight, they were having a girls' night. It was the last Saturday night before Monica's wedding. They were going to get massages, go out to dinner, and then head back to Lizzy's house for dessert and time to enjoy each other's company.

As Jenny picked out a nice pair of jeans and a pretty sweater to wear that evening, Ryan stayed protectively in the room. "Jenny, are you sure you'll be okay with going tonight?"

"I guess it doesn't really matter if I am or not. Monica's my best friend. I *have* to go."

"Jenny, you need to remember this isn't Lizzy's fault."

"*I know that!*" Jenny yelled at Ryan. The shout startled Ryan and tears welled up in his eyes.

"Jenny, you can't let this anger ruin you. God will bless us. He will. I know He will."

Jenny started crying yet again, and let her body go limp in Ryan's arms. "I just want to be a mom. I want to be happy again. I'm tired of this pain so deep in my soul. I thought that baby was ours, Ryan. I really did."

"Me too, honey. Me too."

Despite the emotions that consumed her while getting ready, Jenny arrived at the Monica's house on time. They drove to the salon for their massages and while the masseuse helped Jenny's body relax, she did some praying. "Dear God, I know this is not Lizzy's fault. Please, help me reconnect with her tonight. I do not want to allow this anger to become bitterness." It had been the first time that Jenny had really prayed about her anger, and she could almost instantly feel God healing her heart. For the first time in weeks Jenny felt a glimmer of hope, that maybe, just maybe, she would get through this.

At dinner, as they munched on thick pieces of Italian bread slathered with large pats of butter, they chatted. Lizzy was very quiet and very guarded about what she added to the conversation. She was sensitive to Jenny's emotions, and for the first time Jenny saw that. They had been sitting next to each other in the booth, and Jenny reached over and squeezed her friend's hand. "I'm getting better," she whispered. "I'm sorry."

Lizzy looked at her, smiled her typical nurturing smile and said, "I know dear. God's going to do a great thing in you. I just know it."

Their entrées arrived, and everyone had consumed so much bread and salad it was all they could do to even start eating the delicious pasta dishes in front of them. About five minutes in, the ladies flagged down the waitress and asked for boxes. There was no sense in stuffing themselves since dessert at Lizzy's house promised to be delectable.

As the waitress brought the boxes, Jenny felt her phone vibrating in her purse.

"Why is Ryan calling me on a girls' night? He never does that," she pondered. Figuring it must be important, she excused herself as she took the call in the hallway near the restroom. "Ryan, is everything okay?"

Ryan, who was panting on the other end of the line said things were more than okay. "Missy called. She called. There's two, two of them. They are five. They are waiting for us."

"Ryan? What are you talking about?" Jenny was desperate to make sense of her breathless husband's sentence.

"Twins, a boy and a girl. They are five. Missy wants to know if we will take them?"

Jenny squealed with delight. "Yes! Where do I go?"

"Just come home. She will bring them here," Ryan said excitedly.

Jenny, now as breathless as her husband, hurried back to the table, made arrangements for Monica to ride with Kate, and hugging each of the girls first, headed off.

"Wait, Jenny," Lizzy called.

Jenny looked back, and her friend waved her back over to the table. "Let's pray first, okay?" She smiled at her friend, and came back, sat down, even if only for the brief, forty-five second prayer. With her friends' blessings, she walked out the door and entered her brand-new life. She was going to be a mom!

35

Jenny had admitted that when she heard they were getting the five-year-old twins, that perhaps they were getting an easy end of the deal. After all, five-year-olds are potty trained, sleep through the night, and can follow directions unless, of course, you have been neglected for most of your short life. The twins, who had now been with her and Ryan for five days, were completely disheveled when brought to their home. They had gone through several lice treatments, many changes of pants a day, and Jenny was sure no one had slept more than two hours at a time. The children, who had been malnourished, looked more like three-year-olds, and were constantly hungry.

Their names were Jacob and Emily. They were quite attached to one another, and spent many hours a day huddled in the corner of the couch together. Sometimes, they even sucked on each other's fingers. Each meal that was fed to them and each bath that was given helped bridge a gap. Jenny struggled with wanting to just cuddle them all the time, but sometimes they would much rather just sit alone, holding tight to the sibling that had been their constant companion.

But, today, day five, Ryan was able to stay home from work. The four of them had to venture out in public for the first time as a family. The task at hand was simple enough: to find Jacob and Emily dress clothes to wear to Monica's wedding. The celebration was only two days away, and Missy had assured Jenny that events like a wedding were great for building a family bond.

As Jenny tried to explain to the children what a wedding was, she was met with blank stares. Not easily discouraged, Jenny smiled and said that it was a big party where people got to watch people start a life together. They wore pretty clothes and promised to love each other forever. Emily, despite her rough start in life, was quite perceptive.

She looked at Jenny, "Will this be our wedding? Are you going to love us forever?"

Jenny stopped right there in the middle of the mall, got down on her knees in front of the twins, and said, "Yes. I promise I will love you forever." Ryan, realizing the importance of the moment, followed suit and in a truly reverent voice promised his devotion to these children as well. The four of them embraced in a group hug, sealing the deal. The moment was interrupted by a wet stream running down Jacob's pants, but the parents had already learned to come prepared with extra changes of clothes and many wet wipes to cleanse the children with. The crisis was dealt with swiftly. A small tuxedo was purchased for Jacob, and Emily twirled around in a myriad of dresses. Jenny finally settled on a pretty lavender dress that had sparkles on the bodice and a big poofy skirt. The little girl came alive in those dresses, and her eyes looked genuinely happy as Ryan and Jenny admired her beauty. It was a day Jenny planned to journal about. She wanted to cherish this day forever.

36

Monica slipped into bed, exhausted, excited, and hopeful. Her wedding was only a short sixteen hours away. The rehearsal dinner had gone well, despite the chaos of the week. Words could not express the wholeness she felt standing up at the front of the church, looking into Jer's eyes, Mandy at her side, and her four best friends standing behind her as bridesmaids. Throughout the week, they had all been running scattered. They would flip-flop from Jenny's house to Monica's, helping with everything from last minute alterations of Mandy's flower girl dress, to preparing meals for the newest additions over at Ryan and Jenny's house. Jer had been remarkable all this time, handling the crises that just kept popping up everywhere this last month. He remained calm for her when she couldn't do it herself.

She smiled when she thought of Lizzy, and how her arm was finally uncast. She pictured Kate, glowing with almost seven months of pregnancy under her belt now. Jenny had a different kind of glow about her with her new role in motherhood. She was busy, but she was handling it well. Monica was actually quite impressed with how Jenny and Ryan had stepped up to the plate. It was an overwhelming task taking on those two kiddos, but even the toughest moments seem to leave them in a trail of gratitude. And then, Blair, sweet, faithful, encouraging Blair. Through all of the trials they had all gone through lately, Blair was ever present. Her life had seemed so normal compared to the rest of theirs at the moment. And Blair, being the servant she was, used that normalcy in her life as a blessing to all the rest. It did not matter if it was combing lice out of a child's hair or baking cookies for a wedding, Blair's servant heart that had been recognized through their Bible study stood out. Monica lifted up her friends in prayer, thanking God for how each one of them had encouraged her along the way to fulfilling her dreams. And as she mentioned the word dream, Jer's face came to mind, and she just whispered, "Thank you God. Thank you for him," as she drifted off to a peaceful night sleep.

When Monica woke up in the morning, she was surprised to find that the peace from her sleep before had followed her into the daytime. She had envisioned herself waking up anxious, edgy, and filled with butterflies. But, just as she had the night before, she just kept saying, "Thank you, Lord," and the gratitude filled her heart with calmness.

The wedding was picture perfect. Mandy looked like a little angel, and Jer could not take his eyes off of his beautiful bride. They enjoyed their very first kiss at the moment they were pronounced husband and wife. It was sweet, tender, and definitely lasted a little longer than most wedding kisses. As if they were at a sporting event, after the couple sealed their promises with a kiss, the crowd went wild. Everyone knew what an incredible day of celebration, hope, and love this was! And no one was going to hold back the enthusiasm this occasion deserved.

After countless poses and snapshots, the bridal party made its way to the reception hall. The small banquet center was filled with friends and family all ready to dance the night away.

After Jer and Monica had enjoyed their first dance, Jer surprised Mandy with a very special dance just for the two of them. Mandy's face lit up and it looked to Monica as if her little girl could not have been any happier. God really had seen them through this, and though life would still have its ups and down, Monica finally felt like maybe she was getting her happily ever after.

Sometime between the Hokey Pokey and the Electric Slide, Monica had noticed that all of her bridesmaids were missing. She asked Jer if he knew where they were. He shook his head and asked if she thought they were up to something. "I'm not sure. I don't think so. I'm not a big fan of surprises, and I'm pretty sure they would not pull something crazy on the day of our wedding." Suddenly Monica started feeling anxious. They wouldn't, would they?

She decided to take a stroll around the room, looking for a husband or child belonging to one of them. Perhaps she could get someone to spill the beans. As she wandered around the room, she saw Ryan. He was entertaining Emily and Jacob. When she went over to Ryan, he would barely make eye contact with her.

"I knew it!" she thought to herself. "What could they be up to?"

"Hey, Ryan, where are all the girls?" she asked slyly.

Ryan did not look up. Instead, he just said quietly, "I'm not sure."

She kept pressing, but Monica did not get any more information out of him. At that very moment, she heard a bit of commotion coming from the kitchen. She walked into there and was amazed at what she saw.

There was Kate, beautiful and pregnant. Just an hour ago, she had been glowing. Now, she was being loaded on a stretcher and they were taking her out of the back kitchen doors to avoid making a scene. As they carried her friend out, Monica noticed all the other girls, bowed in prayer, wiping tears, wearing very worried expressions on their faces. She walked over, and bowed her head with her friends.

Monica had gathered from the prayers and the conversation afterwards that Kate's water had broken about forty minutes before that. She was so worried about ruining Monica's wedding that she begged no one to tell her. Shortly thereafter, Kate had begun to feel lightheaded and they decided to call an ambulance to get her to the hospital quickly and safely. Phil had left the boys in Lizzy's care, and he rode with Kate to the hospital.

The group promised Monica that she should go and enjoy her wedding guests and her groom. If there were any updates, they promised to notify her immediately. They all hugged her and assured her that it was still just fine to enjoy her special day with Jer.

Monica found Jer. She walked over to him, whispered the events of the last hour to him, and then, he hugged her, and took her to the dance floor. While they were sharing an intimate slow dance to one of his favorite songs, he knew no one would interrupt. They used that four-minute song to pray for Kate. Jer soothed Monica's worried soul, and he promised her that God had all of this under control. It amazed Monica how quickly her groom had learned how worrisome her heart tended to be, and how easily he calmed her fears, even the fears that had a very real basis in reality.

The remainder of the reception was lovely and calm. The celebration ended promptly at 10:00 p.m. As the clean-up began, Monica realized that it was quite possible that she and Jer would be leaving on their honeymoon without knowing how Kate and the baby were doing. Jer, just looking at her, knew that was on the forefront of her mind.

After they had hugged Mandy many times and said a million I love yous, they left their reception to head to the honeymoon suite he had booked for them. Instead of going straight there, he decided to drive his beautiful bride to the hospital. He knew that the wedding night activities he had hoped to enjoy would be of little value to his bride if she was worried about one of her best friends losing a baby.

Just as they arrived at the hospital, a text message came through on Monica's phone. It was from Phil saying the baby had arrived, a girl, who they named Hope. The baby, only weighing in at two pounds was tiny. Her lungs were well developed despite the baby's preemie status. "A NICU stay will occur for weeks, but mom and baby are okay," the text had finished. Just as she had read that one, another message came through. "Kate says go enjoy your honeymoon. You deserve it. That's an order."

Monica looked at Jer. "Well, if she's ordering me, I guess I better listen." Jer sighed a huge sigh of relief, leaned over and kissed his bride, who was once again glowing, now that the weight of worry was off of her back. The couple left, off to enjoy their three-night honeymoon.

37

Lizzy looked at the online listing for the hundredth time. She knew the listing she was looking at was Blair's previous residence in North Carolina. She was aware at how difficult the process of selling their home had been. She was also aware that God was at work in a major way in their lives.

Brad had come home about two weeks ago with news of a job offer in North Carolina. The little college that offered him a job was named Brevard. Immediately, Lizzy recognized the name, and the wheels started turning in her head. "Could we really up and move from the town we've lived in all our lives? How would I leave the soup kitchen? Our church? Oh, the girls? How would I ever leave the girls?"

She had mentioned the conundrum to Karlene at the soup kitchen. Karlene stated that she even knew of a soup kitchen in that area that had needed a director. Karlene made it quite clear that she thought Lizzy would be perfect for the job. "Anyone who is willing to continue working at a soup kitchen after what you went through? Yeah, you are perfect for it, hon!"

While the thought of moving made her sad, it also filled her heart with excitement! They were old enough to be established, but still young and healthy enough to do years of service for the Lord. She had never seen Brad so excited for a job opportunity. He was ready to pass on his wisdom about finance to the college students. And, by looking at the pictures of Blair's former home online, she realized how fortunate they had been that the house had remained on the market for the last ten months. She called the realtor listed on the page, made an appointment for Saturday, when they would drive the three hours to hopefully set everything in motion for one of the biggest moves of their lives.

38

lair had just spent the day with Ava over at Jenny's house. Ava loved helping entertain Jacob and Emily while Blair helped Jenny find a new routine of laundry and cleaning. Jenny's house had always been near pristine every time Blair had been there, so seeing it looking so lived in was most amusing to Jenny's friends. Blair had been busy assembling two lasagnas and two trays of chicken casserole to go in the freezer when her cell phone rang.

"Hey, Sam, what's up babe?"

She listened to the good news her husband had on the phone.

"Oh my goodness! Finally! What a relief!"

She paused again, now with Jenny looking at her since her voice contained so much excitement.

"Is baby Hope coming home?" Jenny whispered hopefully. Jenny shook her head and held up her finger to tell her she would fill her in after the phone call.

"How much? Really? After ten months on the market they offered our full price? That's unheard of! Yes! *Yes!* Accept it!"

Blair hung up the phone and shared the news. Someone had finally put an offer on their house. They were willing to pay the asking price, and asked nothing else. Blair could feel the financial stresses finally easing. Sam had sounded amazed, almost as if this was a miracle.

The next day, after church, Lizzy and Ryan invited Blair's family out to dinner. They insisted that they not worry about the price of the meals and that they order whatever they wanted. Ryan, who loved giving, insisted the meal was on them.

Once the ordering of the drinks, a few appetizers for the kids, and their entrees had been placed, Lizzy looked at Blair, reached over and grabbed her hand and said, "Blair, I have some news for you."

"Is something wrong?" Blair immediately asked.

"No, nothing's wrong. Things are just going to be different. Blair, we are buying your old house, in North Carolina. Brad will be teaching there. I will be directing a soup kitchen close by."

Blair immediately started crying. "Lizzy, I can't lose you. You were my first friend here. What about Bible study? What about everything?" Suddenly, she was not as excited about the offer put on the house yesterday.

Lizzy, despite a wavering voice near tears, assured her that friendships you built in Christ truly were strong. Then she really surprised Blair. "And Blair, as far as Bible study goes, I was hoping you would take over leading the group. You and Sam have a wonderful foundation of faith in your life. You have stability, your beautiful children," she said, looking around the table to Ava, Charlie, and Franklin, "a testimony to how much you do love God. Please, don't just say no. Think about it. Pray about it."

Blair heard the sincerity in Lizzy's voice, but could not help but question her. "Lizzy, I know nothing about leading a Bible study."

Lizzy, in the most serious voice Blair had ever heard her use, said, "Leadership is more about being a servant than a trailblazer or a know-it-all. You have all the skills you need. Anything else God will give to you as you need it."

The dinner continued with talk about the new jobs, the old to Blair but new to Lizzy neighborhood and town, the best places to eat out, to shop, and the churches they should give a shot. All of a sudden, Blair stopped and got a huge smile on her face. "Carlee. You will be neighbors with my Carlee. Take good care of her for me. Okay? Teach her about Jesus, just like you've taught me."

Lizzy smiled and promised that she would do just that.

They had spent two hours at the restaurant, eating, chatting, laughing, and crying. Even though the kids were older, they were starting to get antsy and bored with the adult conversation. The group was just getting their bill paid and their jackets on when both Lizzy and Blair felt their cell phones going off. "We are headed home. Come over. Hope needs her family there upon arrival."

The group hurried as quickly as they could. Piling into their vehicles, they drove to the other side of town. They pulled in right after Phil and Kate. The other Bible study members were waiting in the driveway as well. It had been a rough four weeks in the hospital, but baby Hope had finally made her way home. She was still tiny, but she was healthy and strong.

The cumbersome group piled into Phil and Kate's small living room. All together, they bowed their heads in prayer and asked for a blessing on Hope's life and the parents who were committed to raising her in the Lord from the start. Praises went up and they felt the blessings coming down on them. This had been a season of continual change, but they knew as long as they held tight to each other and to God, they would all be okay.

39

It was May. The group had gathered in Lizzy's house for their last picnic before she and Brad moved. The annual get-together was normally held in July, but with the kind of year they had all experienced, a celebration, with everyone present was in order. Lizzy and Brad had shipped most of their belongings off with movers the day before. The only thing that remained in their sprawling living room was the beautiful pink couch. All five of them were squeezed on the strong and comfortable sofa. This would be their fourth annual picture sitting on the hot pink fabric. Lizzy, trying to smile as Brad snapped the picture, could barely handle the thought that this was the last photo she would be in. This couch had been part of changing lives. The five of them had experienced the work of God while sitting here. She knew it was just a couch, but it was a symbol. of newness, of fresh starts, of transformation.

She stood up, turned around, and addressed the other four still sitting.

"Blair, I know how you love the simple things in life. I love that about you. And I know what I'm about to ask you is an odd request, but Blair as you accept the role of leading these amazing women, would you consider taking the couch too?"

Blair looked puzzled at first. Then, she remembered her first time walking through the door. The story of the couch had intrigued her.

The comfort of the couch had welcomed her. The friendship found while sitting there had encouraged her. Since the first time she had sat on that couch, she had gone from a woman who was planning an escape from Bible study to the one who was leading it.

She smiled. "I could think of no greater honor. While sitting on this couch, my life has been transformed."

About the Author

Sarah Rose is a stay at home mom who lives with her husband, David and two children, Micah and Lydia in Northwestern Pennsylvania where the winters are long and the snow is deep. She passes those long months sipping coffee, writing whatever comes to mind, and flipping through magazines.

Sarah enjoys building friendship with as many people as she can, spending time with her family, babysitting, serving her church by helping coordinate VBS and being involved in MOPS. Her family also loves hosting students from Spain each summer. Weekends are spent around the table playing board games or around the campfire enjoying warm summer nights.

When it comes to writing, Sarah loves to write about the little moments often overlooked in life, and she wants to make sure that people learn about God's love and grace when they read her work. Just like the characters in her books, she is surrounded by friends who encourage her with the truth from God's Word and support her through prayer. You can read her blog at smilingsarahrose.blogspot.com.

CPSIA information can be obtained at www.ICGtesting.com
Printed in the USA
BVOW07s1709190814

363132BV00001B/3/P

9 781633 380042